TARA NINA

The Cursed
MacKinnons

Haunted
Laird

A Sensual Erotic
Romance

HAUNTED LAIRD

CURSED MACKINNONS SERIES

BOOK 4

BY

TARA NINA

Haunted Laird

Please be advised this book was previously published in 2012.

It has been revised prior to current release.

All rights reserved
Copyright© by Tara Nina
Cover Art by Syneca of OriginalSyn
Published by T.N.Books

ISBN ebook: 9781734205763

Print: 9781734205770

This book is licensed for individual readership only. No portion of this book may be resold or redistributed in any format by any means, electronic or mechanical, including photocopying, recording, or by any information storage and retrieval system without expressed written consent of the author. If you would like to share this book with another person, please purchase an additional copy for each person. Thank you for respecting the author's work.

This is a work of fiction. Names, characters and events are creations of the author's imagination. Any resemblance to any persons, living or dead, is purely coincidental and unintentional by the author.

To obtain permission to excerpt portions of the text, please contact the author at **http://taranina.com**

T.N.Books
New Jersey
2018

Published in the USA

Thank you for purchasing this novel.

It's the support & love of the readers,

And my family,

That makes my world a better place.

Tara Nina

Prologue

Lynn Woodberry stretched and yawned as she sat upright in the hotel room bed. Total comfort surrounded her. It was one of the reasons she'd chosen to stay at the Radisson Blu while in Edinburgh, Scotland. She'd taken the red-eye from Dallas, Texas to London then hopped the first flight from there to Edinburgh. She was checked into her room by eleven and crashed for a nap by noon. Now rested, she scooted off the bed and walked to the window, opening the curtains. The late afternoon sun warmed her face.

The view was magnificent. Ancient stone-faced buildings lined the street. Edinburgh Castle sat off in the distance. The fading sun gave it a haunting outline of red and orange hues and she couldn't help but sigh at the glorious sight. Though she saw it with her own eyes, she still couldn't believe she was finally fulfilling their dream. Her vision blurred as loneliness washed over her, producing a single tear she quickly brushed away. Now was not a time to cry but to rejoice in the closing of the final chapter on a perfect love story and opening the first chapter on a new beginning.

Breathing deep, she refused to let sadness consume her but couldn't stop the flow of thoughts. They were supposed to be on this trip together. But three years ago, life played a cruel joke and took Eddie from her in a horrific car crash. She squeezed her eyes tight trying to flush that tragedy from her brain. It was quiet times like this that made her miss her husband most. Her heart still ached for her high-school sweetheart and soul mate.

For years, they'd planned this trip, plotted their course on a map and saved so they could explore the myths and ghosts of the mystical world of Scotland. She still pictured them together at the kitchen table hunched over travel brochures, maps and books chocked full of ghostly tales from Scotland.

Lynn willed her nerves to calm. She could do this. She could and would fulfill this dream and complete the final chapter on the life she'd shared with Eddie. She needed this trip and knew she had to do it alone. Though her sister suggested she accompany her, something deep inside implied she needed to do this by herself to prove she was ready to move forward, instead of forever mourning the love she'd lost.

Opening her eyes, she lifted her gaze heavenward and prayed for strength. Warmth surrounded her in an invisible hug as it always did when she prayed while thinking of Eddie. In her heart, she knew he watched over her and protected her. This was his way of letting her know he was still around. For some reason, she couldn't see him and it tore at her soul. She could see every other ghost, specter or apparition that lingered trapped between worlds.

But not Eddie. Was the reason she couldn't reach him because he wasn't trapped between plains? Did he rest in peace? She desperately wanted to know.

She sighed deeply, battling the urge to cry and simply crawl back into bed and stay there for eternity. It boggled her mind as to why she couldn't see Eddie. She felt his presence, knew he was near, but couldn't see him or speak with him, though she'd tried. She'd even visited several supposed clairvoyants but their efforts had failed. Lynn huffed at her stupidity, doubting they were even what they'd claimed. Hopefully she'd learn something from this trip as to how to locate and speak with a departed loved one. Maybe someone here knew and could show her the way to complete the spiritual connection.

Lord knows those clairvoyants only showed her how to empty her purse. She was certain there were real medians out there but so far she hadn't found one. Eddie had believed in the spirit world and helped nurture her ability of sight, seeing things that others could not, such as ghosts. She hugged herself.

Eddie taught her the meaning of truly being loved. He was the peaches in her cream. A shiver shot down her spine at the memory of him calling her, his *creamy delight*. Just thinking of how he completed her caused her cheeks to warm and brought an unstoppable smile to her lips. And oh Lordy, their sex life could've filled an erotic novel. Lynn chuckled under her breath as a sensual sensation warmed her from the inside out.

Nope. She had to make this trip in order to complete her memory of Eddie and their incredible love story. Some people called it closure, but not Lynn. It was just the final chapter in a phenomenal romance. If she was going to ever learn how to communicate with beings on the other side, Scotland was the place to do it. Seeing them was one thing, but having a conversation with them was entirely a whole new adventure. One she was ready to embrace.

"I can do this," she whispered to no one in particular, while secretly hoping Eddie's spirit heard her.

Seeing the tour bus pull up outside the hotel, she realized she needed to get a move on. The itinerary for this tour was set and she didn't intend to miss one moment. A quick glance at the clock let her know the bus would leave in thirty minutes, with or without her. Tonight's tour — the underground vaults. She couldn't wait to see them and hear the tales of the ghosts who roamed that underworld.

Chapter One

By the time they finally took a break, Lynn had heard enough. The three men bickered worse than a group of old women sitting around with nothing to do but complain about what ailed them. She still couldn't believe one of them was Fin, Travis' partner at MacShain's Guided Tours, the tour company she'd employed to explore the greatest haunted locations in Scotland. If she'd known one of them was a kidnapper, she never would have joined their group.

Travis! Where was Travis? He'd completely slipped her mind. What had they done with him? It made her stomach churn not knowing if her new friend were dead or alive. Though she'd listened closely to every word they'd said, they never mentioned what happened to him. And she had been so intent on fighting them when they took her captive, she hadn't noticed if he lay unconscious or in a pool of blood at their campsite.

She fidgeted but couldn't move much being they'd tied her hands and feet, then secured her to a makeshift litter with the sleeping bag from her tent that they'd wrapped thick tape around until she was wedged tight. All she could think when she looked at the contraption they had her in was one word. Papoose. She was being hauled up a mountain in a giant papoose. They'd covered her mouth with a piece of the same tape so she couldn't scream. Though she tried, she couldn't push it off with her tongue or wiggle her lips enough to loosen it.

So she resolved herself to lie there, listen, and reserve her strength. They were bound to make a mistake and when they did, she planned to use it to her advantage and escape.

Fin had hidden his face at the campsite she shared with Travis, by keeping his hood tucked low over his head so she didn't get a good look at him then. Now he didn't even try to hide from her as she glared at him while he carried the foot end of her prison. The other two, named Lonnie and Timothy, she couldn't see well from her position. One of them was at the head end of the litter while the other apparently led the way. From what she'd overheard, she was beginning to piece together some of what they were up to, but still didn't understand why it involved kidnapping her.

What did they want with an American from Texas?

If they planned to ransom her off, the joke was on them. Her family wasn't rich. The only surviving blood-related member was her sister, who was married to a small town pharmacist and they had a set of triplets. Definitely no money left there. Absently she shook her head. As to her, when Eddie died, he left her comfortable but not extremely wealthy by any means. If she lived frugally, which she did, the money would last for years. So as far as exchanging her for money, they were out of luck, but she didn't think they had taken her for money. There was this one thing they spoke of several times.

Who or what was this *brotherhood* they mentioned?

Lynn inhaled deeply through her nose. Apparently this brotherhood wanted something they were willing to pay steeply to obtain and didn't care what methods were taken to get it. These guys were out of their minds if they thought she had anything of worth for this brotherhood. She doubted it was her they wanted. It sounded like something was hidden somewhere on this mountain. If they thought she knew where it was, they were crazy.

Unless... She scrolled through everything she'd learned so far. What if they were after something in the cave Travis was taking her to visit? Had they captured her as a trade-off for the cave's location? Did they think that particular cave held whatever it was they were looking for? Did they think Travis shared the coordinates with her and she'd be able to lead them there? Questions tumbled through her head as she swallowed the lump of growing fear in her throat. She didn't know anything. She closed her eyes, wishing she'd never taken Travis' offer to introduce her to a ghost.

She lay there reliving the conversation she'd had with Travis several nights earlier. She must've looked like the biggest sucker going sitting across the table from Travis at a pub after their tour of the underground vaults. Lynn inwardly reprimanded herself for hanging on to his every word as he'd shared his tale of a night he'd spent in a cave with an ancient Scotsman's specter. Travis claimed he would take her there and she'd be able to communicate with a ghost. The one thing she had yet to achieve in all her years of seeing apparitions was actually speaking with the dead and somehow he'd figured that out and used it against her.

Had he noticed her reactions to the lingering souls wandering the vaults? There had been so many, she felt certain she hadn't been able to suppress her excitement from her facial expressions. Had he read her desires and played her for a fool? Throughout the tour, she'd noticed Travis seemed to watch her more intently than any of the others. At the pub, he'd explained he'd been waiting for the right person with which to share his spiritual find. She'd fallen for it completely and even did her best to assure him she was the one he needed, a true believer in everything paranormal.

Was he somehow a part of this whole kidnapping ploy? Lynn shivered inwardly. She hadn't thought of that before. Was Travis not really her friend but an instigator in this ruse to capture an American? She couldn't think straight as ideas of subterfuge and dastardly deeds tormented her thoughts. No! She refused to believe ill of Travis. He was innocent in this whole scenario.

Damn! The predicament she'd managed to get herself into all in the name of ghost chasing. This addiction of hers was finally going to get her killed.

"Lonnie," Timothy griped, loudly. Lynn stirred from her musings and concentrated on their conversation, hoping for a thread of information she could use in her favor. "We need a break. Carryin' this chick up the mountain isn't easy."

"Yeah," Fin chimed in, "when's your turn to help carry her?"

"Quit your grousing," Lonnie snapped. "We don't have much farther and we'll be at the campsite."

"This better be worth it," Fin stated heatedly. "The society offered a tidy sum. How do we know this brotherhood will keep their promise? The society will pay, there's no question there. But this brotherhood seems a bit shady to me."

"You've pointed that out before, Fin. How many times I got to tell you?" Lonnie's growing frustration was evident in his tone. "Me an' Tim helped save Brother Leod from a fire at a club in London. He promised to make us rich if we joined his group."

Lynn felt the foot of the litter lower as Fin set her down. He moved to stand face to face with Lonnie, who now stood near her shoulder. It was apparent he was the one in charge of this operation. She sensed the tension between them. *This* was something she could use to her advantage. Fin hadn't spoken much during the week of her guided tour through the haunts of Edinburgh. He'd let his partner, Travis, handle all the tour guide stuff while he drove the bus. Now he didn't seem to hold his tongue.

"I just find it mighty strange this Brother Leod knows so much about the clan we swore to protect."

"*We*," Lonnie screeched, leaning to within millimeters of Fin's face. "I don't know about you, but I took no oath. It was a fairy tale, a myth handed down from our forefathers that suckered us into believing in a curse on a clan that no longer exists."

"It must be some truth behind it or why would so many before us stand together united?" Lynn saw Fin's stance change as if making ready to fight. "And best o' all, why would this newfound friend o' yours be so interested in what the society protects? Think maybe he's up to no good?"

Lonnie shook as he waved his hands in the air in frustration. "I think you be backing out on us, Fin. You're in too tight with the society." He poked Fin in the chest with his forefinger as he bellowed, "Are you with us or are you no? You might want to be thinking about it afore you answer." He nodded toward the side of the path that was a steep drop-off into a ravine. "Looks to be a mighty long fall."

Fin's shoulders tightened and it appeared as if he reined in his anger, taking a step back. She heard his heavy exhale as he replied, "I'm in."

"Good," Lonnie spat back at him. "Now pick up your end and let's get going."

Lynn couldn't help but wonder about Fin's connection with these two.

Silence fell between them, which gave her time to sort through the limited details. Apparently they all belonged to some sort of society sworn to protect some nonexistent clan. Lonnie had a mysterious new friend with lots of money and a desire to own something the society protected. But what? None of them had let that slip.

Fin wouldn't look at her. Instead his gaze seemed to glance occasionally behind him as if expecting to see someone there at any moment. Travis maybe? Momentarily a spark of hope for his safety gave her an instant of relief that Travis might be tracking them or gone for help. When Fin wasn't looking behind, his eyes stayed straightforward and she could only imagine the hole his glare would bore through Lonnie's back if he had such a power.

And from what she'd figured out, Timothy did whatever Lonnie told him to do. So even if Fin had changed his mind about being a part of this team, he was outnumbered. She focused on Fin. He was the weak link. Something didn't seem right with him and this little adventure. Something she hoped she could twist in her favor when the time was right.

It was after dark when they reached the designated campsite on the ridge. Tents were already erected. It appeared as if they had set up camp before they invaded her campsite and took her captive. They set her down. Timothy stacked wood in the pit to build a fire. Fin disappeared into one of the two tents. Lonnie plopped onto a large rock beside the pit.

When Fin came out of his tent carrying a lit lantern, she tried to talk against the tape to get his attention. Though it was nothing more than a mumbled noise, he squatted beside her and set the lantern on the ground near her head. In a low tone, he spoke to her, "I'm going to remove the tape. If you scream, I'll have to put it back. You're not going to scream are you?"

Lynn shook her head and he slowly removed the tape from her mouth. She wiggled her jaw and wet her lips. It felt good to have that off her face. Now if she could just get him to unwrap the tape that bound her to the stretcher and release her arms from behind her back her shoulders would be forever grateful.

"Can you untie me please?" she asked softly. "I need to go to the bathroom."

Fin glanced at his partners then pulled out a pocketknife and started cutting the tape. He hadn't gotten far when Lonnie jumped up and ran over to him.

"What the hell are you doing?"

Fin didn't stop. He continued cutting without looking up from his task. "The lass is in need of a bathroom break."

Lonnie commanded, "Then she's your responsibility. Make sure she doesn't get away." He turned on his heels and stomped over to the other tent and went inside.

"Real friendly guy," Lynn stated coolly. Fin smiled at her wisecrack and the tension in the back of her neck eased. Once he freed the tape from across the sleeping bag, he lifted it off her and helped her sit upright. After cutting the tape binding her ankles, he untied the rope from around her wrists.

"You okay to stand?"

"I think so. I'm a little stiff."

"Here, I'll help you," Fin offered as he took her hands and guided her to her feet.

Lynn's legs were fine. She wiggled her toes in her boots trying to loosen the tightness in her ankles. Rolling her shoulders and moving her fingers helped relieve the dead sensation and numbness in her arms and hands. The small of her back ached from lying on her hands balled beneath her. The only good thing from being carried up the mountain, she'd laid there listening, learning their motives and reserving her energy. As soon as the tingling quit in her arms and feet, she knew she'd be ready to make a break for it.

She took a step toward the trees when Fin cut her off. "Nay, lassie. I've got to keep you from running." He held a longer rope, which he secured around her waist.

"Really," Lynn said with her eyebrow cocked and a hand on the rope.

"It's either this or I hold your hand while you pee," Fin stated point-blank. Lynn opened her mouth to protest then shut it. He was serious. He grabbed the lantern and held it out so she could see where she was going.

They walked several feet away from the tents. Fin stopped her and turned her to face him. He hung the lantern on a branch so it bathed the area in a low glow. He took hold of her hands as he spoke in a whispered tone so only she could hear.

"Listen, Lynn. Things are not as they seem. Please abide by Lonnie's rules for now an' I'll see to it you make it home safe."

Lynn swallowed her excitement. She was right about Fin. He really wasn't part of this, but somehow had gotten roped into it. Keeping her voice low and her tone even she asked, "Why are you helping them?"

"That be a question I cannot answer now." He nodded toward the campsite. "You best be doing your business quickly or Lonnie just might come looking for us. He may not be the brightest but he does have a mean streak."

She nodded and scooted behind the trees out of his view. Indecision warred within her as she relieved herself while at the same time loosening the rope. She wasn't a liar, she really had to go but she had no intentions of missing the opportunity to escape. When she stood and secured her jeans, she turned and walked face first into a hand over her mouth and an arm around her waist.

"Don't scream, Lynn. It's me, Travis," he whispered in her ear.

Fear filled her. In her panic, his words didn't register. She bit his hand and kneed him in the family jewels. Adrenaline rushed making her run faster than she'd ever run in her life. Limbs slapped her face and left behind stinging scratches. Darkness surrounded her, only the occasional light from the stars and moon filtered through the canopy of trees. Limited line-of-sight didn't stop her. She kept on running. Several times she tripped and miraculously she managed to stay on her feet, blindly grabbing hold of branches or trees to break her fall.

Voices echoed behind her making her push onward even though she gasped for air. Her lungs hurt. There wasn't an uncovered patch of skin that didn't burn from being attacked by objects in the dark. She knew if she didn't slow down she was going to get severely injured. When she couldn't hear the voices behind her anymore, she slowed to a stop and bent over with her hands on her knees trying to clear her head and breathe.

Wheezing in and out, she thought she was going to be sick even though her stomach was empty. Her capturers hadn't fed her. Dizziness made her head spin, causing her to crumble to her knees. Uncontrollable tears gushed and for the first time since the whole thing started, she felt completely helpless. Sob after sob croaked from deep inside her before she finally curled into a ball on the soft forest floor.

She lay there for several minutes more, trying to calm her frazzled nerves. The sensation of warmth cocooned her, soothing her, clearing her thoughts as the faint sound of her dead husband's voice flowed inside her head. *Think, Lynn. Think. There's got to be a way out of this. Lying on the ground won't save you.*

Lynn sat upright, dried her eyes and gathered her wits. Eddie reached out to her in her time of need just as he'd done whenever she was down or distraught over the past three years. This she knew in her heart. Whether she imagined it or not, it was his whispered words of encouragement that sparked her drive to survive and pulled her back together. He was the reason she'd come on this trip to Scotland, to fulfill their ghost hunting dreams. She'd be damned if she'd let some two-bit kidnappers ruin her life. She struggled to her feet and straightened her clothes as best as possible.

Up ahead through the trees, she thought she saw a break in the woods. Maybe there was a meadow and quite possibly a house with people who could help her. Slowly she worked her way in that direction. The sound of male voices from somewhere behind her scared her. They were still coming after her and getting closer. She dug deep for any energy she had left and ran.

The moment she cleared the tree line, the ground went out from under her. She landed on her backside and began a torturous slide, bouncing off saplings, rocks and underbrush as her speed increased. Afraid she'd break her neck if she didn't stop, Lynn kept grabbing onto anything that would slow her descent. Several times the thin saplings she managed to grasp pulled out of the soft ground, slowing her some but not much. Digging in her heels helped, but the moist soil gave away until she hit a solid mass, a well-embedded rock that stopped her downward spiral.

Lynn came to a bone-jarring halt, leaning into the side of the mountain and praying the rock beneath her feet didn't pull out of place. Once the dirt around her stopped shifting, she evaluated her condition. It didn't seem as if anything was broken but it was hard to tell through the total body numbness. Breathing deep, she calmed her overwrought nerves and forced her trembling hands to search from side to side for anything that would help support her. Peering down the length of her body, she realized she'd slipped into a ravine and from her position, it looked bottomless. It wasn't an open meadow she'd seen, it was simply an optical illusion caused by the way the moonlight played upon the countryside.

Damn! She closed her eyes and it hit her. She was living the dream she'd had the first night of this ghost hunting adventure. Dead tired from hiking into the Grampian

Mountains, cozy and warm in her sleeping bag, her imagination ran wild in her sleep and she'd awoken all hot and bothered by the images fired to life in her brain. Thinking back, it replayed as if she were asleep and the dream reoccurred.

Don't look down, whispered through her head as she gasped for a full breath. She clung on for life in her dream just like she did now. Dirt slipped from the mountain, crumbling around her with any movement. Lynn kept her eyes closed tight, listening to the echo of a rock as it rolled into the deep crevice beneath her. It sounded so far away. She tried desperately not to think on the what-if-she-fell scenario and let the memory of the dream temporarily control her thoughts.

She'd had help then whereas now there was none. As she'd reached upward, a hand had grabbed hers. If she remembered correctly, warmth had shot down her arm as a strong hand wrapped around hers. Lynn leaned back into the mountain, letting the vision of hope live in her mind in a valiant effort to relieve the tension of her reality.

One hand held hers, while the other reached and grabbed her backpack, tugging her into the mouth of a cave without so much as a grunt from the effort. Once certain of her safety, she'd lifted onto her knees, turned on a flashlight she couldn't remember from where she'd gotten it, after all it was a dream. Several seconds passed before she could actually focus. When she did, she couldn't believe her eyes.

A gorgeous hunk of a man dressed in full-scale, ancient Scottish regalia stood staring at her. The way the light played across the plains of his face gave him a dangerously rugged appeal. She couldn't decide if his eyes were green, blue or a mixture of both. A firm jaw held a set of perfect male lips. Waves of dark hair thick with amber highlights hung loose about his broad shoulders.

He was bare-chested except for the leather strap that crossed from left shoulder to right hip, which held the sheath for the sword she saw the handle of above his shoulder. The man's abdominal muscles were unlike any she'd ever seen. Ripped was the only word that came to mind, but even that didn't do him justice. A red and green plaid kilt slung low across his hips lay perfectly to his knees. Laced boots covered from his calves to his toes, but from the snug fit hid nothing about their musculature. His legs befit the rest of him, muscles on top of muscles.

For a split second, *wonder if he's true to his kilt* flashed inside her brain and she'd had to fold her hands together to resist the temptation to lift the plaid and take a peek. She swallowed hard, then forced her brain to work and made her mouth form a sentence.

"Thank you for saving me." She remembered speaking as she held her hand out to him.

He'd stared for what seemed like an eternity before he reached for it and helped her to her feet. She stumbled on weakened legs and fell against the solid wall of male flesh. His arm wrapped around her waist, holding her closer along the warmth of his form. His other hand's fingers gently touched her chin and guided her face upward. He seemed to study her before his eyes met hers.

The low sultry baritone of his words washed over her as he spoke. "Nay, milady. 'Tis ye who hath saved me."

In the dream, his arm tightened around her waist as he lifted her without any effort. One of her hands held his thick, bulging biceps while her other hand landed on his waist for support. Never had anyone lifted her to *kiss her*. Nerves fired to life she'd thought were dead. The closer his lips got, the more she wanted his kiss. This slow motion event was killing her. The heat of his breath caressed her lips just millimeters apart. The warmth of his body set her on fire with desire.

Lynn caught herself craning her neck trying to reach his lips. Opening her eyes, reality set in. She truly clung to the side of a mountain for life. She tilted her chin upward, but saw nothing much in the darkness. Was there a handsome man waiting to rescue her? Nervously she laughed at the ludicrous thought. There wasn't anyone who knew where she was or would risk their life to save her.

This wasn't a dream. This was her reality.

No, it was up to her to save herself. She dug deep, brushing away the perfect hero-saves-the-day dream from her thoughts and struggled for survival.

Cautious in her movements, she inched along the rock, turning until she was face first against the dirt. Should she try to climb down or was it easier to go up? Lynn moved her hands palm flat along the ground searching for any point of support, anything she could grasp. The fingertips of her right hand brushed something rough and solid. Lynn rotated her head in that direction. It appeared to be a ledge. God, she hoped it would hold her.

With slow, careful movements, she worked her way toward the lip in the rock, hugging her body to the mountain for dear life. She used the plants for leverage, holding on but not pulling so their roots wouldn't break and jerk free from the ground. It seemed like an eternity had passed before she reached the ledge. Every muscle ached and trembled but she refused to give in to the exhaustion that threatened to tear her from the mountainside. Nope. She didn't plan to fail. That ledge was her salvation, her place to rest and recuperate until sunrise.

She gripped the rocky edge. When it didn't break off and slide away, relief made her smile. Now all she had to do was pull herself onto it. Toeing her boots into the dirt, she tried to push upward using her legs. The ground slid from beneath her right foot and she slipped, leaving her dangling by her hands. Her shoulders screamed in pain and her arms shook, but she tightened her grip refusing to lose this battle.

Sheer will helped her find a sturdier foundation. Her left foot located a rock and her right she planted between the base of a bush and the dirt. Spread-eagled wasn't the best position but it kept her from falling any farther. The rock didn't feel as sturdy as the bush so she pushed up on her right leg and glided her left leg closer to the right until it found a secure spot stuck in a hole a wee bit higher than the bush. She struggled inch by inch until she was able to hoist herself onto the ledge.

Lynn rolled several feet away from the edge and onto her back. Breathing heavily, she lay still trying to evaluate her condition. Nothing felt broken. Her legs and arms trembled from the excessive exertion she'd placed on them. This definitely was more exercise than she'd ever gotten. Seconds turned into minutes as she simply lay there. The pounding of her heart resumed its normal pace and the tension in her body relaxed, giving her a chance to reflect on the events that led up to her precarious predicament.

Don't scream, Lynn. It's me, Travis.

The words rolled around inside her head and the sudden realization of what she'd done surfaced. *Ohmygod! Travis!* She'd attacked Travis, the one person who she thought was on her side. Or maybe he wasn't. She truly didn't know for sure anymore. Hysterical laughter rose from her chest.

What had she done?

She rolled onto her side and curled into a ball. The laughter slowed and exhaustion took over. Everything hurt. Both arms and legs trembled uncontrollably. A deep-seated ache bloomed from her core and spread outward until every ounce of her was thoroughly saturated, causing her muscles to spasm at will. Her exhausted condition gave her no other choice but to sleep. If she saw the morning light, it would be a miracle.

Invisible, strong, gentle hands caressed her, lulling her to sleep. Warmth surrounded her. The handsome man reappeared in her dreams, giving her comfort in her time of need. She snuggled closer into the imaginary heat of his body. He surrounded her, cuddling her against him as if he alone would protect her from the elements. Sensing he stood watch, Lynn relaxed further into the depths of sleep, letting his sexy image renew her desire for life and for him.

He appeared to be tall with wide shoulders and thick arms that would hold her for as long as she needed to be held. Long, dark hair with rich shades of red was pulled away from his face, making her wish to untie what bound it and set it free to landscape his rugged features. Deep, blue-green eyes stared at her filled with wonder and wisdom beyond his years.

In this dream, he said nothing nor did she. He simply held her while she slept, keeping her close and away from the edge of the ledge. His imaginary heat warmed her and warded off the cool night air. A sensual dream guided her into a peaceful place where the hazards of her day no longer existed. It was just her and her hot, dream-walking man.

Chapter Two

Cupping his bruised balls, Travis quickly hobbled behind a tree as someone with a lantern hurried after Lynn. It had to be the throb radiating up his middle that crossed his eyes and had him seeing things. That couldn't have been Fin going after her. He repositioned his damaged goods and sucked it up. Lynn had been kidnapped and for some unexplainable reason, Fin was involved.

Someone had knocked him out earlier and the back of his head still pounded. Now combined with the stabbing pain from his balls, Travis was hornet-sized mad. There was only one way to find out what the hell was going on and it didn't entail tending his wounds like a little boy.

Travis took a step then halted for a second to listen. A male voice called out to Fin from the campsite. Knowing where Fin was, Travis quietly sped after him. He had to reach Lynn before any of them. It was his fault she was in this predicament. The dim light from the lantern stuck out in the otherwise dark of night. He tracked the bobbing dot deeper into the woods. Voices echoed behind him, but he doubted they'd catch up anytime soon.

When the light stopped for a second, Travis made his move. Travis lunged from behind and wrapped up Fin's legs, causing him to fall face forward. The lantern rolled under a bush. Luckily it was battery powered and didn't cause a fire. Without giving Fin a chance, he flipped him over, straddled his waist, grabbed his shirt and hauled his arm back, fist ready to pummel his face.

"Wait," Fin gasped, "I'm on your side."

"Really," Travis remarked sarcastically. "From where I see it, you're helping the bad guys. You need to be giving me a mighty fine reason not to be bloodying your nose right about now."

When he took a swing at Fin's face but intentionally missed, Fin reacted, bucking and twisting throwing Travis off-balanced just enough for Fin to land a blow to Travis' cheek. Stunned Travis froze glaring at Fin. If they'd been at home, Fin's bucking beneath him would've made him hot. Now it only made his balls hurt more.

"I can't believe you just did that," Travis sputtered. "I never would've actually hit you."

"You gave me no choice." Fin grabbed Travis' wrists. "I know about the ghost you saw last time we were camping."

Travis jerked his wrists free and absently dropped his hands to his side and released his grip on Fin's shirt. He didn't remember telling anyone but Lynn about his experience. How did Fin know? He slid off Fin to sit beside him. "How'd you know about that?"

Fin sat up. "I found you lost in the woods around dawn babbling incoherently about what happened. It took a bit of coaxing to get it out o' you but even then you only gave me bits 'n pieces. When I finally put it together, I knew you'd found it."

"Found what?"

"The cursed MacKinnon my ancestors swore to protect."

"The who of what?" Travis couldn't have hidden his confusion if he tried.

Several yards away, the sounds of two people stumbling through the woods and calling Fin's name had them both jumping to their feet. Fin clasped Travis' shoulder.

"I don't have time to explain right now, but you've got to trust me on this." He released Travis with a quick, tender kiss to the spot he'd hit on Travis' cheek, bent and scooped up the lantern. "You find the lass.

I'll guide those two in the wrong direction. We'll meet at our favorite campsite just north o' here as soon as possible. Just find the lass before anything happens to her."

Before Travis could reply, Fin ran toward the sound of Lonnie and Timothy. Travis gave Fin a few minutes to make sure he was telling the truth. When the light stopped for what seemed an eternity, the echo of arguing voices floated through the air. Being too far away, he couldn't make out exactly what was said but got the gist of it. Fin was considered to be an idiot by the one. Travis grinned. That's where the one was wrong. Fin was anything but stupid. Travis wasn't sure what Fin had gotten himself into but he'd asked him for his trust in this matter. When the light moved, leading the band of three away from Lynn's true direction, Travis believed in his best friend and lover.

Travis spun on his heels and hurried after Lynn. With the help of a flashlight palmed in his hand to shield the light, he tracked her. It was obvious from the broken branches and smashed plants on the ground, she ran wildly through the underbrush. Even a blind man could follow her trail.

Finally standing at the edge of the ravine, he froze. Checking his compass, the realization of where he stood slapped him as if it were an invisible hand to his face. Images from a night he wished he'd never experienced flashed to life inside his brain. He and Fin had been camping not far from this spot. He glanced over his shoulder in the general direction of where Fin and the others camped and knew Fin picked that spot intentionally. If it were a few hundred yards north, it would be the exact same campsite, their favorite campsite.

The sensation of rolling downhill uncontrollably washed over him. Sweat beaded his upper lip. His chest tightened making it difficult to breathe. In a drunken stupor, he'd wandered away from camp. At first, he imagined he was tracking a massive buck with a prize trophy rack. The farther he got from camp the more he lost his concentration and sense of direction. The excessive amount of drink he'd consumed hadn't help. His thoughts muddled and his vision was unclear. He miss-stepped and the next thing he knew he was at the bottom of the ravine.

Ass over teakettle, he flipped, slid and rolled, hitting everything in his path. He couldn't say how long he laid on the ground before he realized he needed to get up. Nothing made sense. All he could figure out through the ale-confused fog wrapped around his brain was that he had to climb to get back to camp. No matter how hard he tried, he couldn't remember the exact details of how he ended up in a cave.

He just did.

Images of him on his back with some strange, ancient-looking, transparent dude hovering over him sent an ice-cold chill through his veins. Even now he shivered from the strength of the memory. Staring down toward the ravine made him dizzy so he stepped back several feet. He needed to pull himself together. His newfound friend, Lynn, needed him. But he knew it would be foolish to go over the edge in the dark. One slip and it could mean a broken neck and what good would he be to her then? How would he help her if he were dead?

Oh, god! Was she dead? He returned to the edge. Holding on to a tree for support he pointed the beam of his flashlight into the darkness. A definitive skid mark stood out marking her descent. He swallowed hard against the lump in his throat and prayed for her safety. He needed to think this through and plan his next step in finding her. Travis scanned the night sky and knew sunrise was several hours away and from the pattern of dark clouds in the distance, a storm was on the horizon. Damn! He'd have to hurry.

What he needed was a way to scale the side without falling. Then it hit him. Lynn had been tied with a rope she'd removed when she relieved herself. He'd seen the rope and knew she had to be the one tied to it. From her position behind the bush, he knew what she was doing and had given her some privacy until she was finished and started to run. Thinking back, he wished he'd approached her differently. She was scared and hadn't realized it was him who had his arm around her and his hand over her mouth. Travis regretted that move.

He took off his pack and hid it. Without it, he could make better time back to the rope. His only hope was that it was forgotten and still lay where it had been dropped. The closer he got to their campsite, the louder the voices became. Fin was the object of their anger. They hadn't found the woman and it was all Fin's fault, because he was supposed to be their expert guide.

Travis worked his way closer and remained hidden as he watched. Fin sat quietly on a rock just taking the verbal abuse from one of the men. The man yelling lifted his hand as if he were going to smack Fin. That got a reaction out of Fin. He sprang to his feet and leveled the man with a solid two-handed shove to his chest. Before the guy could move, Fin was on top of him with his knee in his stomach, and his collar fisted tight, lifting the man's shoulders several inches from the ground.

"Don't you ever try 'n strike me again. It will be your last mistake." Fin shoved him hard against the dirt as he stood. Staring at the man, he spat out, "We start the hunt again at first light. I told you these woods swallow people whole at night." He stomped toward his tent. Travis made sure only Fin saw him for a split second then melded into the darkness again. Fin shot an evil glare at the pair over his shoulder and in an ominous tone added, "There're creatures out there that feed on human flesh. If'n I was you, I'd seek shelter before they find you."

Taking his cue from Fin's words, Travis made a horrific growling sound low in his throat and threw a rock into the bushes behind the campsite. Fin disappeared into his tent. The other two couldn't move fast enough, stumbling over each other to get into their tent. It was all Travis could do not to break out laughing at the sight. As soon as Fin appeared at Travis' side with his gear in hand, they hurried away from the campsite, but not before Travis gathered the rope.

"I sort of found Lynn," Travis stated the second they were far enough away to not be heard.

"What do you mean, sort of?"

"She went over the ledge into the ravine. I needed the rope to follow her."

"Damn," Fin replied on a hurried breath as they increased their pace.

They had to find her and somehow do it before the other two grew a set of balls and came out of their tent. They reached where he'd stowed his pack just as the skies opened. Driving rain and high winds caused them to seek shelter.

Luck was definitely not on their side.

* * * * *

Lynn woke to the sound of rain, yet she was dry. A fuzzy sensation tickled her nose. Warmth cocooned her making her feel safe. Prying her eyes open, she came to the sudden realization she was covered with a blanket. She bolted upright letting the blanket drop to her lap as she stared wide-eyed at it. It appeared to be an animal skin of some sort. She was guessing deer maybe. It was soft to the touch. But she had no idea where it came from.

Slowly, she stood. Every ounce of her balked in rebellion and made her feel a hundred years old. Lynn stretched and turned then stopped as she realized her location. The mouth of a cave had been her shelter from the elements. If she hadn't been so worn out and it hadn't been the dead of night, she might've found this and slid farther in for more protection rather than lay in the opening. She stepped through the entrance. Lynn walked several feet then came to an abrupt halt.

An apparition stood in her path. Clear as day, she saw him. The ghost stood a few inches taller than she, wearing the garb of an ancient Scotsman. A knee-length kilt, knee-high boots, a long-sleeved shirt tied together in the front with a neatly woven string and a sash wrapped around him from his left shoulder to his right hip. He had the essence of a proud warrior, which exuded in the air around him. At first sight, she thought he was the sexy visitor from her dreams, but as she studied him further, she realized he wasn't.

Excitement stirred to life and filled her with warmth. She hadn't been wrong to follow Travis on this ghost hunt. Right before her stood the chance she'd been waiting for, the opportunity to learn how to communicate with the spirit world. In all of her adventures to haunted locations with her late husband, Eddie, she'd never spoken with a ghost. She'd only seen or felt them. Her stomach churned. Maybe now she'd discover how to locate and speak with Eddie.

Deciding there couldn't be two caves in the area with a ghost inhabitant, she took a chance. Lynn gathered a smidgeon of her Texan charm, extended her hand and did her best not to sound scared. The sight of her dirty hand made her realize she must look a bit worn as she absently rubbed her hands on her muddy jeans, patted her unruly curly hair then extended her hand again.

"You must be Jasper." She held her breath and hoped he'd communicate with her.

If she surprised him with her statement, it didn't show in his expression. He floated around her, studying her from head to toe. Cool air swirled engulfing her, making her shiver. She dropped her hand to her side since he didn't seem to have any intention of shaking it. He took a stance of intimidation with his arms crossed over his chest, legs spread hip distance apart and a stern look upon his face.

"How do ye know my name?"

Lynn relaxed, letting go of the breath she held. Excitement made her heart pound. Somehow she'd ended up where she was supposed to be. Call it dumb luck. Call it anything you liked. She found Jasper and the cave that Travis was supposed to be taking her to visit. Travis hadn't lied to her after all.

"I'm Lynn," she said, hoping to start a conversation with him. Questions scooted excitedly through her head at a rapid rate. This was her first actual ghost to person discussion. She breathed deep doing her best to focus and slow the whirlwind of need-to-knows from confusing her thoughts. A step forward made Jasper float backwards keeping a safe distance between them.

She cleared her throat and tried again. "I'm a friend of Travis."

It looked as if a weight lifted from his shoulders when he spoke, "Where is Travis? How did ye find me without him?"

Not sure what she should say, she carefully chose her words. "Travis and I started this trip to see you together but we got separated. I fell and slid into the ravine. It was only when I tried to climb back to the top that I landed on what I thought was a ledge. I didn't know it was your cave until now."

He seemed to study her as if trying to decipher whether she spoke the truth or not. His chin tilted and his gaze softened. "Did ye rest well?"

She glanced at the blanket and realized where it must have come from. "Did you do that?"

He nodded then waved his hand, causing the blanket to float into the cave. He dropped it onto a pile of assorted things.

"Thank you. That was very kind of you."

"I could no let ye freeze, now could I. It would no be the chivalrous thing to do." He said it in such a matter-of-fact way it almost made her laugh. But that wouldn't be polite so she swallowed it.

"Jasper, why is it you haunt this cave?" Lynn asked. Deciding she would be less intimidating to him if she sat, she moved to the closest large rock and took a seat. She wanted to gain his trust and learn why and how he remained trapped between plains. Desperately she wanted to know if there was a way to communicate beyond the veil with those who had passed into the other realm.

He appeared hesitant to speak. He leaned against the wall opposite from where she sat. "For o'er two hundred years I have called this cave my home. I swore an oath to protect a friend."

Jasper floated to stand at the mouth of the cave and appeared to be watching the rain. Lynn moved to his side. The side nearest to him was kept cool by his essence. She sensed a deep sadness within him. When she tried to touch him and console him, her hand passed right through his arm and made her shiver for a second. She shook off the instant chill and followed her train of thought.

"This friend." She paused, trying not to pry but needing to know. "Did you love this person?"

He didn't answer her question. Instead he stood straight and stiff. Without looking at her, he turned. "I 'ave felt it on the wind. Nature whispers to me o' a change that needs to come."

When his gaze met hers, she read his loss and sensed his desperation. Whatever was happening was not of his choosing.

"Come," he said solemnly as he floated toward the rear of the cave. "'Tis time ye met my friend."

Lynn followed without saying a word. A mismatched assortment of lanterns flickered to life as he passed and she got the feeling he did that for her. She doubted he needed the light they radiated to see where to go. The rear of the cave became three different sections. One went off to the left. There was a huge middle opening. The third was to the right. Jasper hovered for a second then turned to her.

His eyes closed and the most wonderful verse in an ancient tongue left his lips. She listened but did not understand. Knowing she stood in Scotland and he was from a time well past, he had to have spoken Gaelic. When his eyes opened, she swore she saw a single tear that disappeared instantly.

"Jasper, that was beautiful," she said breathlessly. "What does it mean? I don't understand the language in which you spoke."

He smiled then cupped her face in his hands. There was no actual contact. She only sensed his touch. Extreme cold penetrated all the way to her core. When he spoke the words again, she understood.

> *"Thy quiet son awaits.*
> *Within a chamber deep.*
> *Safe an' sound he shall sleep.*
> *'Tis a place he loved.*
> *High above thy game ravine.*

Never ta be seen.

Sheltered from thy nature's fury 'n a burrow o' her makin'.

Lest ye nay be 'n a hurry.

Three choices tease thee.

Two be wrong.

One be right.

Choose well an' set him free.

Choose wrong an' face thy wrath o' me."

The cold left her body the moment he let go. The passage was beautiful except for that wrath part at the end. That part made her take an extra second before speaking again. He tried to hide it but she knew he held deep feelings for the person he protected. Carefully she dissected each sentence.

"Why did you hide the quiet son and who is he?"

She held his timid stare. When he spoke, she paid close attention.

"My best friend, Padon MacKinnon, fell to a curse. He an' his six *brathairs*—brothers—were turned to stone by an evil man carrying a black book o' dark magic. MacGillivray made a pact with the devil, he did. He placed this curse then disappeared. When Akira, their *piuthar*—sister—

discovered a partial anti-curse, she feared for their safety. Rumors MacGillivray would return an' destroy the statues flourished. Akira took no risk with her *brathairs*. She gathered everyone she knew her *brathairs* trusted and swore us to a task."

She watched his face closely. This was a man crippled with grief and guilt. Jasper sank onto a rock. His specter looked frail and worn as if the weight of his world still rode on his shoulders.

"What kind of task?" Lynn asked quietly, hoping to help ease his pain by talking.

"She gave each o' us a *brathair* to hide an' protect. We were to write a riddle that gave clues to their sanctuary an' give it to her."

"That's what you just recited for me," she said.

He nodded. "She placed them 'n a diary. Nay but one person knew the answers an' it was not her. She did not want to have both riddle an' answer together. It was up to us to pass it along to a family member an' swear them to secrecy should something happen to us." His shoulders sagged.

"Did you pass the answer to another?"

"Nay," he replied in a somber tone, "I did not. I kept him secret, giving only the riddle to Akira."

"Is it because you loved him that you did this?" Lynn must've touched a nerve because he leapt to his feet.

"Padon was closer to me than a *brathair*." His voice shook as he spoke. His hand fisted over his heart. "'Tis my fault this happened. If'n I were there MacGillivray would not have gotten into the castle an' the curse would not have happened. Clan MacKinnon would not have ended 'n such an evil manner."

And there it was, the reason for his guilt. He blamed himself for what happened to his friend and his family. Jasper floated upward, spinning around as a horrific screech left him. Lynn covered her ears against the din resonating off the walls. When she located Jasper levitating near the ceiling, she knew from the sight of him, he was a broken man when he died.

A man in love with another man. That must've been tough during the time when he lived. Now it's accepted, but back then, she couldn't be sure if they would've been ostracized for their actions. It was something of which she had no knowledge. She didn't doubt love between men happened throughout history; after all, the men of today' didn't invent it. They just were apt to admit it more freely.

"Jasper, how can I help?" she asked in the most tender and caring tone she could muster across the knot in her throat. This was a love story that time forgot.

He floated down to face her. "Ye can set Padon free." He turned and waved a hand gallantly in front of all three openings. "Choose wisely."

With his hand fisted over his heart he stared directly at her and waited. The pressure was on. Which did she choose and what would he do if she chose incorrectly? Oh yeah. His wrath would fall upon her. Damn. Why couldn't this be simple with a bright red flashing arrow pointing the way?

Bright. Red. Arrow.

Lynn glanced over her shoulder at Jasper. He hovered behind her in a stoic stance with his hand fisted over his heart. She turned face forward and let the grin split her lips. He was practically broadcasting where he'd hidden his friend. She looked at the left, then the right and made her choice. Shoulders lifted, back straight, she walked toward the left opening and heard him hiss ever so lowly to the point if she wasn't paying close attention, she would've missed it. Not skipping a beat, she grabbed the lit lantern off the ledge beside the opening then turned and marched directly into the center tunnel.

Several feet in, the sound of running water whispered in the air. Coolness filled each breath. Lynn held the light and took each step carefully. After her harrowing experience down the side of the mountain last night, she had no intentions of miss stepping again and ending up Lord-knows-where.

The ground was soft and moist causing her boots to sink a little. She swung the light around inspecting the area. It seemed to be very damp and wet and the sound of running water echoed even more loudly. After a few more minutes, she reached a slight drop that appeared to be naturally made steps. She tested each one before placing her full weight upon it. At the bottom, she continued following the sound of the water.

She walked around a bend and a wondrous sight met her eyes. A waterfall cascaded from the ceiling into a huge pool of water. Dimmed rays of the rainy morning sun snuck in through holes here and there in the roof. Nothing could ever be more pristinely beautiful. Untouched by anyone, preserved by nature. Lynn spun around taking it all in until she saw him.

Lynn hurried to the statue of a man tucked off to the side in an alcove. She set the lantern on a rock and simply stared. He was the biggest, hulk of a man she'd ever seen. Dressed in only a kilt and nothing else. A pair of large hands held a sword poised to strike. Strong legs held him in a lunge position as if he'd started to attack but was halted instantaneously. Taut muscles rippled his massive chest, abdomen and back. His mouth hung open. His scream lost for eternity in time. The surprised anguish in his face tugged at her heart.

Here was a warrior prepared to kill or be killed. Instead, he'd been cursed.

She felt Jasper's presence behind her. "Can ye help him?" His voice came across as a whispered plea tearing at her heart.

"What can I do?"

Jasper floated to stand between her and the statue. "Ye must speak the words o' the anti-curse at the fall o' night to free him."

"Why have you not done this?" Curiosity gripped her. If there was a cure then why didn't Jasper free him? There had to be a catch.

"In the words o' Akira, 'tis only half a freedom." He turned to face the statue, lifting his hand to cup the distraught face of his friend. Lynn dug deep to keep from crying at the sight. "Man by night 'n stone by day. They've only now found a way to free him completely."

Lynn sniffed against the threat of tears. "They? Who are they?"

Jasper returned his gaze to hers. "Akira and the *brathairs* who hath been freed."

Puzzlement made her brows purse and boggled her mind. If there was a way to free him why hadn't the others come here to help? Why did he need her to do it? Staring at him, something hit her and she couldn't believe she hadn't asked him earlier.

"Jasper, when did this curse occur?" He looked at her funny as if confused. "What year did this MacGillivray recite this curse that froze your friend in stone?"

"Seventeen hundred an' forty."

She stepped back and sank onto the nearest rock. Jasper was caught between dimensions for over two hundred years. Did he know what year it was? Did he understand the concept of time?

"Milady," Jasper stated as he curtsied. "I am aware o' the length o' time I hath stood guard. My only regret is that I did naught to prevent this from happening."

Though it startled her he seemed to have heard her thoughts, she asked, "How did you find out it was time to set him free?"

"On occasion, I ventured to Castle MacKinnon an' hid an' watched, waiting for any word o' how to save him. I felt it was my duty to watch o'er Akira as well." A grin brightened his features. "The lass no be o' need o' help. She be a strong one an' knew how to handle this mess. Still I accepted it as part o' my duty to watch her from afar. On one o' my visits, I was surprised to see Gavin an' Ian had been freed."

He paused as if gathering his thoughts. "It stunned me to see them 'n the light o' day. I came back here to think. I prepared to question Akira and returned. When I arrived, she had a visitor. The spirit o' Mary Campbell o' Breadalbane had come 'n search o' Akira. I lingered an' listened to every word. The secret they shared be forever etched 'n my memory."

"This secret, will it set him free?" she asked, even though she suspected she knew the answer.

"Aye. But only 'n the night. By day he will return to stone. We have to get him to Castle MacKinnon to find out how to free him completely."

Lynn pursed her lips. Her gaze lingered on the statue. Was this really a man frozen in time in a casket of stone? Did she believe the story? She looked at Jasper and considered the source. She believed in ghosts, had seen them nearly all her life and now she'd actually had a conversation with one.

Yep, she decided. This story had merit. It had to be real. Travis believed Jasper's story so much he convinced her to come here to meet the ancient spirit. She smiled.

"I'll help you set him free."

Chapter Three

Ceum saor de clach
Be Ye Biast air duine
'Tis Gaol dara slighe
Ge Ye be mèinne
Dh'oidche mur dh'là

The words at first she thought were beautiful were now giving her a pounding headache as she tried repeatedly to get them right. Though Jasper worked diligently with her, she knew she tried his patience because he disappeared several times for a matter of a second then reappeared at her side. She guessed he needed a chance to gather his calm before continuing. It had to be her Texas twang that kept twisting the enunciation and screwing it up.

It annoyed her to a degree that every time she questioned him about contacting the spirit world, he redirected the conversation. Deciding if she did as he asked and learned the verse then maybe he'd be more cooperative with what she wanted to know in return. She spent endless hours with Jasper trying to learn the Celtic verse she needed to recite at sundown.

Completely frustrated, Lynn snapped, "Why do you need me to speak the words? Why can't you do it?"

Jasper sat back. Sadness darkened his gaze. "Because I no longer live."

He disappeared and Lynn hated she'd asked him in such a harsh manner. She concluded a flesh and blood being had to speak the anti-curse. When Jasper reappeared, she apologized, "I'm sorry."

"It be all right, lass. Ye be tired and thy verse be hard for one with no background in Gaelic."

Lynn kept her voice even and polite as she asked another question that had plagued her thoughts. "Why didn't you have Travis speak it when he found your cave? Why did you have him bring me here to meet you?"

"In Padon's case, thy curse need be spoken from a woman's tongue."

"In Padon's case, a woman's tongue." Her brow pursed as she questioned him. "What do you mean by that?"

When her stomach growled loudly, it gave Jasper an excuse not to explain and changed the subject. Jasper apologized profusely for being an unforgivable host for not providing supplement for his guest. He'd shown her to the collection of knapsacks and assorted camping and spelunking equipment he'd compiled scaring people out of the cave over the centuries. She plundered through several of the more modern backpacks and acquired pre-packaged airtight meal rations, a cup and a spoon.

The food wasn't the tastiest, but it was sufficient to stave her hunger. Drinking water from the fresh underground stream helped wash down the rations. Lynn sat quietly soaking her feet in the cool water and staring at the statue.

Was he alive in there? Could he hear them? Did he know they were there? These were questions she stored away to ask him once he was free from his stone prison.

Lynn shrugged off her shirt, stood and shimmied out of her jeans. In her bra and panties, she rinsed the mud from her clothes then laid them over a rock to dry. Though she'd washed up some earlier, she desperately needed to cleanse away more of the grim from her fall. She hesitated when she reached around to unhook her bra.

"Jasper, if you can here me," she called out, "I'm going to take a bath."

His words whispered down to her. "Ye privacy I shall respect."

A smile cracked her lips. He was the most polite man—umm, ghost, she'd ever met. Even though she knew she wasn't his type, he'd let her know he wouldn't peek. After removing her undergarments, rinsing them and laying them to dry with her other clothing, she stepped into the water. Out of the corner of her eye she spied something drifting down the stairs. Surprised, she turned thinking it was Jasper but instead it was a towel, washcloth and a bar of soap.

"I found these in a pack and thought ye could use them," his voice floated to her ears as the items landed on the ground near the water.

"Thank you," she said, knowing he heard her without having to raise her voice. She scooped the soap and the washcloth into her hand and walked farther into the deeper middle of the stream where it formed a significant pool.

The water was cold but refreshing to her tired muscles. She dunked under soaking every inch, making sure she wet her hair. Rigorously she lathered her tangled mess of curls trying her best to rid it of the debris it gathered in her fall. From the amount of tiny twigs and leaves she removed, she bet she looked more like a wild animal than a woman and wondered why Jasper had even spoken to her at all. Lynn laughed. Jasper wasn't looking at her as a woman but as a means to free the love of his life. She doubted seriously if he'd watched her bathe it would've turned him on in the least.

She wasn't the proper gender to be his type. Lynn smiled, feeling relaxed and strangely safe for the first time in hours. Due to the thickness of her hair, she was having difficulty rinsing out the soap. Seeing the pulsing cascade of the waterfall, she decided to use it like a shower in hopes of removing the resilient suds. Lynn swam over and hoisted herself on to the ledge behind the waterfall. After slipping and sliding a bit, she managed to gain a foothold as she leaned back against the rock wall.

She looked through the thinnest area of the waterfall and focused on the statue. Light from the menagerie of lanterns Jasper had provided shone on the stone surface giving it an oddly beautiful appeal. Lynn felt compelled to speak the verse as she stood in the mist of the falling water.

"Ceum saor de clach
Be Ye Biast air duine
'Tis Gaol dara slighe
Ge Ye be mèinne

Dh'oidche mur dh'là"

Seeing nothing happen, a slight bit of disappointment filled her. She took a breath and leaned her head into the more rapid pulse of the waterfall and rinsed the suds from her hair and body. Lynn stepped back from the stream, brushing the hair and water from her eyes. The moment she regained her focus, she froze. The gasp lodged in her throat.

Was she dreaming?

When he woke, the realization he was no longer at Castle MacKinnon hit him in the chest with an invisible solid blow. What happened? Where was he? And most importantly, where was his family?

Padon stumbled forward with his sword held tightly, ready to strike. MacGillivray was behind this. He felt most certain that dark-eyed Devil lingered near. He swung around trying to gain his bearings. Shock shook him to the core as he recognized his surroundings.

He was in the hunting cave. But how? Last he remembered he was aiming to kill MacGillivray for attacking his *brathairs*. Padon surveyed the area for any signs of life, knowing only he and Jasper knew of this cave's location. Jasper had to be behind his being here.

He shook his head. Had it been a dream? Try as he might he couldn't remember clearly what had happened? Had he been on a hunting trip with Jasper, drank too much and dreamed the whole *brathairs* turned to stone by MacGillivray scenario? The tension in his chest eased a tad but not entirely. He lowered his sword and knelt by the stream, cupping some water for a drink, hoping to wash away the severely dusty sensation from his mouth.

He had barely swallowed when he saw her. A vision most beautiful stood washing her hair in the waterfall. 'Twas it a dream? He splashed the water on his face and blinked but she still remained. How had she gotten here? No woman had ever ventured into their hunting cave.

"Go to her. She is your salvation."

The words whispered to his ears in the sound of his friend, Jasper's, voice. He jumped to his feet and spun around but didn't see him. Anger, confusion and fear mixed within him. What the hell was going on? What sort of sorcery was this? Hearing voices but seeing no one… He slowly turned to the vixen that now stood staring at him from the other side of the waterfall. No one was here but her.

Maybe she had the answers he sought, since Jasper seemed to be playing games with him.

Taking deliberate steps, he shortened the distance. Before entering the water, he set his sword on a large rock and dropped his kilt to the ground. No need getting his only clothing wet while he interrogated the woman. He smiled inwardly, knowing he was no small man and being naked only added to his intimidation strategy. At least that's what he hoped when it came to the weaker sex. Determined to get answers he forged through the water and onto the ledge.

Coming face to face with her, rattled his fierce demeanor. She was not simply a woman, but a gorgeous specimen of female flesh. Though she tried to cover herself with her hands, she failed miserably. He doubted even his oversized hands would hide those scrumptiously large breasts. Taut pink nipples peeked from beneath the arm and hand that attempted to shield them. Instant hunger pitted in his stomach for a sample of their flavor.

Her other arm and hand did its best to cover the treasure between her thighs. It disappointed him to not get even a glimpse of her mound. Would she balk if he removed her hand so he could see? Padon shook off the idea. He needed answers not sex. But his body pleaded otherwise as his shaft stirred to life. The awakening of his senses kept him perusing her attributes and muddled his thoughts with desire.

Though she was short in stature, she made up for it with her incredibly voluptuous figure as far as he was concerned. If her bottom was round and filled his hands, she'd be perfect. Absently he flexed his palms, curling his fingers in and out as if he could somehow feel her there without actually touching her. It didn't help ease the growing tension in his bawls for this woman. Being in her presence made him remember he was a man as his cock twitched and stiffened even more.

Padon forced his gaze to lift from her assets and look upon her face. Its shape was that of a cherubic angel. Auburn curls carelessly framed her features. Her lips trembled and it pained him to read fear in her bright blue eyes. In an attempt to calm her, he reached to cup her cheek but she leaned away from his touch. He dug deep to find his voice and hoped it came across soothing.

"I will nay hurt thee, my wee one. I only ask thee for answers."

Vigorously rubbing her eyes, she couldn't believe what she'd seen squatting at the edge of the stream, drinking water. She shot a quick look where the statue had been to find it missing. A pile of pebbles lay in its spot. Cutting her eyes back to the gorgeous naked hunk, Lynn was bewildered by this sudden turn of events. What time was it? She had no idea. Had the sun gone down and night fallen while she was preoccupied with getting clean?

In reality, she hadn't been entirely convinced the curse existed or that the partial anti-curse she'd struggled to learn would work.

Her eyes widened. The proof it was true stood and marched toward the waterfall. It was obvious he saw her. Lynn's heart pounded. Oh Lord, what was she going to do? Run? Scream? After an unsuccessful attempt to clear the knot from her throat, she knew screaming was out. The closer he got the more her insides twisted with excitement and fear. He looked similar to the man in her dream. Tall, dark, handsome and ready to save the day.

Near the waterfall, he stopped, laid his sword down and released his kilt letting it slide to the ground. Lynn's jaw dropped. He was the epitome of pure male perfection. Thick biceps, a broad chest, ripped abs tapering to a healthy waist held up by a set of strong legs and a healthy endowment sat centered between those muscled thighs. Realizing she stared at his privates, Lynn felt warmth radiate in her cheeks and forced her eyes to lift. Heat seemed to sizzle in the air as she caught his gaze with hers. The masculine shape of his face, wide jaw, firm lips, and the intensity of his blue-green stare made her shiver.

The word perfect didn't describe him well enough as far as she was concerned. Damn! Somehow the man from her dreams had stepped from her imagination and become a real person. He was one hot, drop-dead sexy beast and he was headed her way. Lynn struggled to cover up as best as possible.

The way he cut through the waterfall and lifted with ease onto the ledge in front of her was like one of those extremely sensual TV commercials, where the male model wore next to nothing, except in this case he was naked. Lynn could barely breathe when he closed the distance between them. Beads of water rolled down his glorious chest and it was all she could do not to let her gaze follow its trail lower. It wouldn't be polite to stare and even more wrong to ogle him. She kept telling herself this, trying to control the urge to examine him from head to toe again.

Yet politeness didn't stop him. His ardent gaze caressed her skin like a tender touch sending chills across her flesh. Her nipples hardened and she tried desperately to keep them covered but knew she failed from the heated look in his eyes. Was he a breast man? Lynn shook herself for even wondering about his sexual likes, but it didn't stop her from tingling all over under his avid scrutiny. The sight of his tongue darting across his lips when his eyes lowered to the hand that covered her mound made her instantly wet.

Lordy, what was wrong with her? She'd never reacted this strongly to anyone. But this wasn't just anyone. This was an overtly sexual ancient Scotsman who'd been wrongly imprisoned for over two hundred years. If she thought going without sex for three years was rough, she bet centuries without was horrific for someone as gorgeous as he. Did his parts even work after being asleep for so long?

She chanced a quick glance and was assured it was in perfect working condition. It stood hard and proud aimed straight at her. It took a great deal of resolve to keep herself covered and not reach to touch such a magnificent piece of male anatomy. She wasn't even sure how she managed to hold her hands in place. When he reached toward her face, it startled her and she flinched.

Wrong move. His deep blue-green eyes seemed to darken with concern as he spoke in the softest, richest of baritones with a thick sensual Scottish lilt. Lynn nearly melted into a puddle at his words. He called her wee one. No one had ever called her little. Nope she was far from petite and yet this hulk of a man thought she was small. Heat grew in her stomach and spread throughout her. Damn. He oozed sexual charm from every well-defined inch of him.

Lynn struggled to clear her throat and find her voice, but somehow managed to eek out a single word. "Answers?"

"Aye," he said huskily as he inched closer to her face. "There be many questions starting with how ye taste."

His lips touched hers in a soft caress. This time when he reached to cup her cheek, she didn't withdraw. Instead she leaned into it living in the spontaneity of the moment.

When the tip of his tongue beckoned for entrance, she abided parting her lips and returning his kiss. Lynn couldn't resist. After all, he was the man from her dreams, the one who rescued her when she fell. At least he had in the dream if not in reality. From the feel of his heat surrounding her and the touch of his fingertips, she felt certain he had somehow reached out to her in the night and kept her safe and warm as she slept in the mouth of the cave. This she believed in her heart even if she didn't know how he did it.

For the first time in three years, she felt truly alive inside. Her body reacted to his touch, his taste and the sensual manipulation of his tongue with hers in a sultry dance that stimulated her senses. The man knew how to ignite a fire in a woman with simply a kiss and she couldn't help but enjoy it.

So caught up in the moment, she relaxed her arms from their shield positions and wrapped them around his waist, pulling him closer against her. Just for a second, she wanted to enjoy the feel of him, before she'd do the sensible thing and end their kiss. Her nipples brushed his warm flesh sending chills skittering along her spine. His strong fingers played the muscles of her back, trailing ever so softly downward until he grasped her bottom firmly in both hands, causing her to sigh against his lips. She liked the way he massaged her tush. The more he rolled her flesh in his hands, the wetter she became.

Something whispered she should stop, take a step back and regain her composure. But she was too far-gone, ruled by the raw passionate urges ripping through her core and driving her senses wild.

The rub of his solid girth against her abdomen had her intensifying their kiss as she ran her hands up and down his back. Things were completely out of her command as she relinquished full control to desire. Her hands had a mind of their own, squeezing his tight ass. She couldn't help but mimic the rocking motion of his hips with hers against each other. Breaking from their kiss for air, she grappled for a moment of sanity. But he didn't stop. He hoisted her against the rock wall, positioned her legs around his waist and entered her in one deep plunge.

For a second he halted, placing kisses to her brow while his hands gently rubbed her thighs and bottom. Nuzzling her ear, he whispered, "My wee one, ye hath me out o' control with need. I could no stop. Are ye all right or should we no continue?"

He cupped her face in one hand while the other cradled her bottom as he held her pressed against the rock wall. The I-want-to-fuck-you-but-I'll-stop-if-you-want-me-to look in his eyes tore at her heart. She'd never done anything like this in her life. He filled her, stretching her, making her feel whole again and she wasn't about to stop the wonderful sensation, not now. She'd worry about the consequences later.

Lynn maneuvered one arm around his neck while the other touched his cheek. She held his heated gaze and smiled. "Continue," she said then gathered his lips in a kiss she hoped relayed her needs and wants. She moved her hips, encouraging him to pump in and out, increasing the tension of her impending orgasm. It didn't take much to convince him she was okay and ready to continue.

When she licked his nipple, the growl that emanated from his throat tickled her to the center of her core. She had this gorgeous hunk on the edge and it thrilled her to know she'd done that to him. Pumping faster and faster in tune with him, Lynn's insides tightened and her heart raced. At some point, she realized he'd pulled her away from the rock wall and held her weight fully in his arms while she rode him wildly. He held her as if she weighed nothing and that turned her on even more. Her breasts bounced, rubbing his chest. She held onto his shoulders, digging her nails into his skin, but he didn't even seem to take notice. Instead, he met her beat for beat, filling her on every upward thrust until she finally came.

Lynn screamed in ecstasy as the orgasm roared from deep within, sending moisture washing over him. But he wasn't done. She gasped for air as he drove into her several more times until his juices released combining with hers. The thrum of her inner muscles synced with the throb of his shaft and coaxed her into another, yet mini-orgasm. Never had that happened, ever. Lynn leaned into him, struggling to hang on given the limp nature of her legs and arms. If he set her down now, she'd probably crumble into a pile on the ground.

As far as Lynn was concerned, it may have been hard and fast, but it was mind blowing to say the least. He held her until she urged her legs to move and wiggled them free of his loose grip and slid them down from his waist to stand. They trembled but she managed to make them work and kept herself from falling. Her gaze lowered to the magnificent appendage that had given her such a phenomenal experience. Then it hit her. She hadn't even introduced herself. She'd just gone with the flow of desire and ridden this gorgeous hunk into sexual oblivion.

Oh Lordy, what had she done? He'd just woken from an extended nap locked in stone and she hadn't even given him a chance to recuperate. Did he even remember what had happened that caused him to be turned to stone? Better yet, did he even know he'd been cursed into a stone statue for centuries? Perhaps he thought he'd simply awoken from a deep sleep to find a naked woman ready and willing for sex?

Lordy, Lordy, Lordy what had she done?

She'd acted like an out-of-control hormonal woman in the throes of lust, that's what she'd done. Lynn couldn't meet his gaze though she felt his eyes on her. What was she going to say? Should she apologize for acting on impulse? Heat simmered in her cheeks.

Guilt threatened to spoil the whole thing. Had she taken advantage of Padon? After all, he wasn't her husband, her boyfriend or anything. He'd simply awakened from a curse with a hard-on. But, didn't the average man wake with "morning wood" most of the time? Lord knows Eddie had on many occasions. Eddie! Lynn's heart sank. She'd just cheated on Eddie's memory.

She tried desperately to trample the growing double-dose of guilt by any means that came to mind. It wasn't like her to jump the bones of a stranger, but she did love the spontaneity of what had just happened. In Eddie's words, *sex should be all about the moment. Take it whenever and wherever the mood strikes.* A smile tickled her lips at the memory but was quickly doused.

She stared at Padon's feet, unable to find the right words to say to ease this awkwardness between them or help alleviate the sharp pain within her chest. She'd betrayed her loving husband's trust. When Padon's fingers attempted to lift her chin to look upon her face, she resisted until his words graced her ears.

"My wee one, there be no shame in what we have done. Only joy and mutual pleasure." He crouched until he was looking into her face. The sincerity in his eyes melted her shame with his honest questions. "Did ye no reach your pleasure? Shall we try again until ye do?" A spark of mischief shone in his gaze and in the twist of his wicked grin, forcing her to smile in return.

She'd reached her pleasure all right, several times. Lynn breathed deep shaking off the momentary doubts that she'd attacked him but it did nothing for the sinking feeling she'd somehow befouled her marriage vows. They were adults and adults had sex. Guilt over Eddie threatened her happiness, but looking at the sexual heat in Padon's eyes made her body react.

Rolling her eyes, she knew she was going straight to the devil for the thoughts flicking through her brain. Lynn's conscience battled the renewed lust and required that she at least start a conversation with him and help him adjust to his new world before ride two on the hot-'n-heavy-Padon train. *If* she let that happen again. At the moment, she wasn't sure it was a good idea that sex happened in the first place. She'd gotten caught up in the moment, the sexual spontaneity. She tried desperately to convince herself but wasn't having much success.

Besides, she sighed as Jasper's words resurfaced. Padon wasn't completely free. They needed to get him to Castle MacKinnon if they were to accomplish that feat and if what Jasper told her about the anti-curse were true, he'd return to stone at daybreak. That only gave them the night to travel.

Lynn swallowed as she found her voice. She stood straight and did her best not to show her nervousness or the guilt that had taken root in her soul. "Padon, my name is

Lynn Woodberry. I am from the state of Texas in America."

His brows bunched then glanced around before returning his gaze to hers. "We are in Scotland, no?"

"Yes," she answered then smiled. "I came to Scotland to explore the rich spirit-filled culture of your people and the lands. I met a man named Travis Shain, who told me a vivid tale of a ghost, who lingered in a cave within the Grampian Mountains. That's how I met Jasper and he led me to you."

"Jasper." The single word spoken from his lips seemed to make him remember something important. Padon's gaze widened as he looked across the top of her head. The color drained from his face and Lynn knew before she turned that Jasper hovered somewhere near behind her.

Padon instantly shielded her with his body as he faced the ghostly apparition that once was his friend. His voice shook first with what seemed to be disbelief then quickly switched to anger. "Ye be a ghost. How hath this happened? Tell me and I shall seek vengeance against their soul."

"'Tis a long tale, *m'caraid*." His head shook sadly. "Thy lady be cold. This be a conversation best told beside a fire for her sake."

With that said, he disappeared. Padon gasped as he jerked backwards from the sight, nearly stepping on her foot. Lynn suspected surprise, not fear, caused this reaction. Surprise at how his world had changed and was about to change even more.

Chapter Four

Wrapped in the deerskin blanket, Lynn sat beside the fire Padon built in the main entrance of the cave. It surprised her when he came out of one of the three rear tunnels with a large armload of wood. It seemed he and Jasper had stored a good bit of timber for firewood in there. Most had rotted over time but he managed to salvage enough to burn through the night if need be. For the moment, rain no longer poured buckets of water mixed with wind, but had slowed to a steady, windless downpour. Her clothes were neatly placed across rocks near the fire to dry.

"Aye, Padon," Jasper nodded, starting the conversation once they'd settled around the fire. "I am a ghost. Many years hath passed since ye were cursed. The time is now to set ye free." Lynn heard the hitch in his voice as if he struggled to keep his composure. This was most difficult for Jasper.

Padon's massive hand shoved through his hair tugging it from his face. Confusion riddled his features. Knotting the towel tightly across her breasts and keeping the deerskin blanket draped across her shoulders so together these items covered all of her,

Lynn closed the distance between them and took his hand. Hers looked so tiny in his strong one and she sensed he could break every bone if he decided to close his hand tight enough around hers. Her insides quaked in his presence. His heat surrounded her as she stepped forward until mere inches separated them. Stretching upward, she brushed a determined strand of hair from his eyes and smiled.

"Padon." Lynn liked his name and wished she knew its meaning. "There is much you need to know. But most of all, you have to understand the curse you suffered has lasted for over two hundred years. The man that placed it is dead, but his descendant lives on carrying a deadly hate within his soul."

"MacGillivray," he spoke on a venom-filled whisper.

"Aye," Jasper confirmed, which caused Padon's gaze to lift from hers and stare across her head at Jasper. Padon stepped around Lynn to face Jasper.

He looked around before he spoke. "I was not here when MacGillivray attacked. Ye brought me to the hunting cave."

Jasper simply nodded. Padon's brows pursed as he stared at Jasper. "Ye did not crossover to the Garden o' Angels. Why? Why do ye still linger?"

"I gave Akira my oath o' protection." Jasper's chin tilted and his shoulders squared. Lynn noted he stood several inches shorter than Padon and wasn't as broad but he wasn't a small man by any means. No, he'd held his own in his time, she'd bet.

Padon circled Jasper then stood to face him again. "Ye swore an oath o' protection with my *piuthar*. To protect her?"

"Ye lunk-headed fool," Jasper snapped. "Ye and I both know Akira needed no protection. Thy oath was to protect ye from the wrath o' MacGillivray. He found out about the anti-curse and realized he made a fatal mistake. If anyone spoke it, the MacKinnon *brathairs* would live at night but not by day. It was a chance o' revenge he could not take so he placed a bounty on the statues. They were to be destroyed so ye would never be freed."

"An' nay one soul spoke the words to free me until now." Padon's tone sounded perplexed. "Why? Why not free me and my *brathairs* so we could seek vengeance on MacGillivray?"

Jasper floated around him making Padon's head turn to follow his path. "Akira kept the anti-curse to herself. She said it was only half a life and not fair to her *brathairs*. She gave each o' ye to different trusted clans who swore an oath to hide ye until thy path to total freedom could be found."

"Freedom hath been found?" Padon questioned.

"Aye." Jasper nodded. "We need to get ya to Castle MacKinnon to learn it."

As if fate had another nasty card to play against them, the storm took a turn for the worse. Lightning brightened the night sky. Thunder roared like an outraged lion. Gale force winds and driving rain switched into high gear making it too dangerous to travel so it was decided to wait it out even if it meant staying another day in the cave. Silence fell between them. Lynn moved closer to the fire and snuggled deeper into the deerskin. Words escaped her. She didn't know what to do or say so she didn't do anything but be there for him if he chose to talk.

Hours slipped away and no one had spoken.

Padon absently poked at the flame-licked logs with a long stick. His expression gave away nothing of his thoughts but Lynn figured the story Jasper shared with him had to weigh heavy upon him. When he wasn't squatted beside the fire, he paced like a caged animal. Lynn knew he had to be trying to sort things out for himself. He'd fallen to a curse trying to save his family only to wake in a cave centuries later. That had to be hard to digest so she understood the long period of silence. It had to be his way of handling it. So she waited until he was ready to discuss it with someone. Then she'd do her best to help.

She stood and gathered her clothes. They were finally dry. Her boots were still a bit damp so she left them where they were beside the heat. She walked several feet into the back tunnel out of view but still close enough the firelight helped her see to dress. Coolness coated her flesh and she knew Jasper hovered behind her. It didn't matter that she stepped into her panties and jeans in front of him. She knew he wasn't looking at her and his words confirmed it.

"Do ye think he will forgive me?" Though his voice was hardly above a whisper, she heard him easily.

"Forgive you for what? You did nothing wrong." Lynn pulled on her shirt over her bra then turned to face him. Sadness wafted from him and unlike Padon, Jasper's face hid nothing.

"I was not there to save him."

"Give him time to think things through. I doubt he harbors any anger toward you." Lynn did her best to console the deeply distraught ghost.

"Time be something I no longer have." His head hung low as it shook.

"I don't understand," Lynn said. Confusion pursed her brow. "You're a spirit, you have nothing left but time."

"Nay. Padon be free. My duty here be done. Angels call me home. Time draws near for me to join them in the garden."

Jasper was leaving. Lynn opened her mouth to ask more questions about the afterlife and how to make contact, but swallowed her selfish thirst for knowledge. Now was not the time to pry Jasper for information he had avoided giving earlier. He needed closure and she planned to make sure he got it before he crossed over.

"Now I think I understand the part of your riddle about the quiet son." Lynn changed the subject, trying to uplift Jasper's spirits. If he didn't have long to linger, she wanted to make his last hours here enjoyable and she couldn't do that without Padon's participation.

Jasper snorted. "Aye. Padon never was one to talk about his troubles. He held them close to the heart."

"I can see that. I think he's had time enough to mull it over. Let's see if we can convince him to talk." Lynn's patience had worn thin. Sitting around watching Padon and Jasper avoid each other hadn't been fun. It tore her up inside knowing what she did about Jasper's feelings. She didn't wait for Jasper's reply. It was lost in the air behind her. Now that Jasper didn't have much time meant Padon's brooding session was over in her book.

His friend sacrificed a lot and Padon owed him more than he could ever repay. So she planned to make sure Jasper got his chance to speak his heart before passing over in to the Garden of Angels. Lord knows she carried heaviness in her heart for Eddie. She understood how it drained the soul having unspoken words gnawing at your every waking moment. Lynn paused, closed her eyes for a second shoving her own needs aside and focused on Jasper. He deserved more from Padon. Her resolve reset, she opened her eyes and forged ahead.

Lynn returned to the main opening of the cave and found Padon sitting in the rain staring into the darkened skies. The storm had surged into a powerful hurricane-sized force sending blinding rain, hail and a strong wind whipping into the first few feet of the cave. The flames flickered and hissed as raindrops and wind made contact. He turned his gaze to her, staring at her across his shoulder. Lightning flashed, outlining him in a split second of iridescent glow making him look fierce and angry against the stormy background.

Damn. He looked sexy. Raw emotion filled his gaze as he turned to face her. She read anger mixed with confusion, which she wished she could wash away like the rain did to everything outside. His rain-slicked skin had her wanting to stand beside him, touching his flesh, gliding her hands over every soaked inch. Hair hanging loose and wet encompassed his giving him a wildly uncontrollable appeal. His muscles glistened in the firelight. Lightning bolts highlighting him added an edge of fierceness to his overall appearance. If he had his sword in his hand, he'd make an even more wicked-looking warrior. Lynn's nipples hardened and desire bloomed.

Lowering her eyes weakened her knees. Padon stood in the rain. It was visibly apparent the cold rain did not affect his manhood. She swallowed, grasping for the reins on her lust buggy. He wasn't making this easy. Not with an obvious hard-on.

Think Jasper.

That helped a little. Keeping her thoughts on Jasper took a slight nip in her hunger for Padon, but didn't douse it completely. She doubted anything would ever succeed at killing the exquisitely sexual thoughts he seemed to spur to life in her imagination. When he stepped toward her, tension coiled within her and her breasts ached for his touch. The world around her seemed to disappear, as he became her solitary focus.

He moved with the grace and skill of a well-trained predator. Water dripped from him, running down his wide chest, trickling along his abdomen causing her gaze to follow the sensual trail straight to the bulge in his kilt. Padon closed the distance between them, cupping her face in his hands. He leaned forward, taking her lips with his into a soft, warm kiss. His hands tangled in her curls. He kissed a path to her ear and whispered words that melted her heart as he hugged her close to him.

"My wee one, I need ye to show me the way. I know not the path o' this world." He leaned back, placing a small gap between them. Panic and fear flickered in his gaze if only for a split-second and it nearly floored her to hear him say, "Fear lives within me for the first time 'n my life. I know not what to do."

These were words she didn't expect and it took her a few moments to gather her thoughts. Lynn touched his cheek then brushed a dripping strand of hair from his brow. Holding his timid gaze, she spoke from her heart. "I will help you, Padon. There is nothing to fear. I will help you find your way. Think of this as a new exciting adventure and all will be right in your world."

He touched his brow to hers as he held her tight. "Thank ye, my wee one. Ye be the strength I need to flourish where I would flounder and fail otherwise."

"I doubt you would ever flounder or fail at anything you set your mind to, Padon."

Their lips found one another's, drawing strength and desire through their touch. He rubbed against her abdomen increasing the heat already ignited within her. The kiss turned passionate and it was all she could do to end it.

Think Jasper.

The words whispered through her brain and forced her to pull from the wonderful tastiness of his mouth. "Padon," she said huskily against his lips, "Jasper's time is short. The angels call him home. There is much you two need to discuss before he leaves."

"Umm." Padon sighed. "Ye be right, my wee one. He be the reason for much o' the turmoil within me."

"I know." Lynn smiled at him. "Go to him. Talk. Listen. Enjoy the last few hours he has to spend. Remember the good, not the bad."

Padon released her and brushed a finger down her nose. "How did ye get so smart?"

Lynn straightened her shoulders and grinned. "I'm a woman. We're born that way."

His laughter rolled around the cave causing her to laugh along with him. With a well-placed kiss to her cheek, he turned and walked into the tunnel at the back of the cave. Lynn knew they needed some time alone so she picked up the deerskin blanket and made her way to the fire. Looking down, she shook her head at the damp state of her clothes and wondered if she'd ever be dry again.

Right before the sun came up, Lynn followed the sound of their voices and found them hanging out by the stream. She lingered on the natural stairs and watched, feeling like an intruder but couldn't help but admire the pair of friends. They were laughing and carrying on as if nothing had ever separated them. She eavesdropped and heard a funny story shared between them that had her covering her mouth trying to stifle her laugh.

She failed. Jasper called to her. "Come join us, lass. We are but reminiscing about ole times."

Lynn moved to sit on the opposite side of Jasper facing Padon. "I'm sorry. I was curious as to how you two were doing."

"We be fairing very well," Jasper stated then smiled. His eyes shone brighter than ever and Lynn sensed his happiness, but couldn't help but wonder if he'd spoken the truth of his heart. Jasper's smile faded as he met her gaze and shook his head giving her the answer. He hadn't. How he knew her thoughts still amazed her but she ignored it and focused on the issue. He needed to state his case if he were to rest in peace. This she felt strongly about to the point she almost spoke but the pleading distress in Jasper's eyes kept her mouth shut.

So she changed the subject and looked at Padon. "It's almost sunrise. The storm seems to be stopping so hopefully, tonight we can take you home."

"'Twill take more than a night to reach Castle MacKinnon," he said, clearing the laughter from his throat. "Unless ye have fast horses waiting for us, it be a long trek by foot."

Excitement bloomed in Lynn's chest as she remembered the car she and Travis drove and left at Fin's grandfather's farmhouse when they'd started this trip to meet Jasper. All they had to do was reach that car located about a mile from the base of the mountain and Padon stood a chance at getting home more quickly.

Thinking of Travis, she said a silent prayer for his safety and that the storm had caused Fin and his crew to flee the scene, especially since she'd escaped. With any luck, karma would bite them in the ass and get them back for what they'd done to her and Travis. Lynn tamped down the sudden need for vengeance and focused on the mission at hand. Once Padon was safe, then she'd pay a visit to the local authorities and tell them about the kidnapping, leaving out the tiny detail about why she was camping in the first place. They really didn't need to know she was ghost hunting.

She gave Padon a lifted eyebrow look as she teased him. "I have something faster than a horse. But we still have to make it from here to a farmhouse on the other side of the mountain in a night."

Her heart sank knowing it had taken her and Travis a full day to reach the campsite where she'd been kidnapped. It was at least another half a day's trek up the mountain tied to the litter. If her calculations were correct, there was no way they'd reach the car in the span of a night. A thought sprang to life. Maybe it had taken that long because she and Travis were weighed down by the backpacks and her kidnappers were slowed because they carried her. Without the added weight, she and Padon should be able to travel faster. Before she could share this news, Padon stood.

A strange look crossed his face. He reached for his sword. Holding it in both hands, he grimaced and a pain-riddled roar escaped. An electric sizzle heated the air as Padon returned to stone.

Lynn's jaw dropped and her eyes widened. Though she knew it was supposed to happen, she still couldn't believe it. Right before her eyes, the magic of the curse took away Padon's freedom.

Chapter Five

Within hours of the storm passing, Travis was scouring the mountainside in search of his friend Lynn. He and Fin tracked Lynn's path until the storm had become too fierce then took cover to wait it out. Everything they'd found pointed to the fact she had gone over the edge into the ravine, but it was unsafe to follow until the rain ended. As he descended, it didn't look good for the lass. What was left of her trail showed she'd slid quite a ways. Travis couldn't be sure if this was anywhere near where he had fallen months ago. Though the images sporadically shot through his head, they didn't give any clues to the cave's exact location. He knew in his gut, it had to be in this general vicinity.

He'd been the first to go over the side, following the brutal path of Lynn's fall. He stood on a rock giving him a chance to steady himself and survey the area for any evidence of her. Below him there were no further signs of her sliding all the way to the floor of the ravine. But the rain could've washed them away. From what he could decipher, she seemed to have simply vanished at this point. Looking up he thought he saw something, but from this angle it was difficult to see.

Shielding his eyes from the rising sun, he spotted the ledge and telltale signs Lynn had ventured in that direction. He scaled up and over until he managed to reach the ledge with the rope and Fin's help. Peering over the edge, he saw nothing. No Lynn and most of all no Jasper. The knot in his gut let him know he was in the right place.

Travis landed with a thud inside the cave. He couldn't believe he actually stood here again. Untying the rope from around his waist, he tugged on it sending a signal to Fin. He leaned, gripping the wall of the cave and yelled, "I found the cave. Come on down."

The rope disappeared. He knew it was a matter of time before Fin made his way down the mountainside. He stood quiet, listening, hoping to hear her voice. Dying embers from a fire simmered in a round stone pit. Someone had been here or was possibly still here. Hope sprang to life that his friend was alive. Slowly he moved deeper into the cave.

The pile of items Jasper had collected over the years sat to the left just like he remembered. Hanging on a root that stuck out of the cave's wall was his leather flask. Travis lifted it, removed the cap and took a whiff. His nose crinkled at the memory of that dastardly drink which tainted his luck. He placed the cap back on and returned it to its proper place. When he turned, his foot tangled in a deerskin blanket and he tripped and fell into the pile with a loud crash.

So much for being quiet, he snorted as he untangled himself from the mess and stood. Fin landed with a catlike precision on the ledge with a knife held tight in his hand. He shrugged as he met Travis' curious gaze.

"I heard a noise and didn't know what happened. You never know what you might run inta 'n here." Fin grinned as he tucked his knife into its sheath on his hip and untied the rope. It was a good thing he still had a hand on it when Jasper suddenly flashed into the cave.

Thrown off-balanced, Fin nearly toppled backwards over the ledge. Between his grip on the rope and Travis quickly running to his aide, he managed to regain his footing. Travis tugged him close and gave him a quick kiss to the tip of his nose. "Don't scare me like that," Travis stated as he let him go once he knew Fin was safe. "Bad enough you had me believing you'd gotten tangled up with that good-for-nothing pair."

Fin's wide-eyed gaze and sudden gaping jaw cut off his babbling, letting Travis know exactly where Jasper stood in the cave. He turned and came face-to-face with the being who'd haunted his dreams since that fateful first meeting when Jasper gave him the task of finding a woman who believed in the unbelievable and bring her back here. That woman was Lynn. He'd never thought to question why Jasper needed a "true-believer" as he had called it. Travis had simply followed orders out of fear. Not seeing Lynn, he wondered why the ghost needed a flesh and blood woman and what had he done with her if indeed she'd made it into this cave?

"Hello, Jasper," Travis said in as even a tone as he could muster and hoped his fear didn't show in his voice. He desperately needed to know if Lynn was safe. If not, he'd never forgive himself for bringing her into this without first questioning Jasper's motives more thoroughly. As it was, she'd already been kidnapped and fallen into a ravine. She could even be laying at the bottom somewhere bleeding to death for all he knew. He needed to make this conversation with Jasper go smoothly and quickly, because if she wasn't here he needed to hop over the ledge and continue the search.

"Travis," Jasper replied with a nod of his head in Fin's direction. Suspicion filled his transparent features and his stance was one of caution. "Who hath ye brought along with ye?"

Travis introduced Fin. "This is my best friend and partner in business and in life, Fin MacIntyre. We're looking f—"

Before Travis could ask about Lynn, Fin cut him off. He stepped beside Travis, took a knee and bowed his head. "Aye, Sire. I be eternally 'n awe o' your service and pledge my allegiance to you in the protection of Clan MacKinnon."

Dumbstruck, Travis leaned sideways staring at Fin as if he'd lost his mind. They'd been friends since they were young and lovers for years, but he knew nothing of this side of Fin. It took him by surprise to hear Fin pledging his allegiance to someone, especially a ghost. He didn't tear his eyes away from Fin until Jasper spoke.

"MacIntyre." He seemed to mull over the name for several long seconds. "My *piuthar* married a MacIntyre. Be ye o' her descent?"

"Aye," Fin answered without looking up.

"Stand, sir. We must speak."

When Fin complied, Travis opened his mouth but couldn't form any words. The sound of a woman clearing her throat had both him and Fin looking toward the rear of the cave. Jasper simply floated to a collection of several large rocks and took a seat. Relief washed over Travis as he ran to greet Lynn with Fin right beside him.

"Lynn, lass, you're all right." He tugged her into a bear hug then immediately started checking her for broken bones.

"Travis," Lynn said with an embarrassed giggle as she wiggled out of his reach. "Really, I'm fine. Honest, I'd tell you if I thought anything was broken. Bruised but not broken." She flashed him a smile, holding her hands up as if to prove her point.

He stepped back, giving her some room though he wasn't completely convinced she wasn't hurt. "That was a hell o' a fall you took. You sure?"

Lynn nodded fervently. "Jasper took care of me." It was then she caught sight of who was with Travis. "Fin? Travis, are you aware he was one of the kidnappers?"

"Aye, he knows," Fin answered. "I told you it was not as it seemed. You just needed to trust me."

"Did you know this was going to happen ahead of time?" Bewildered, Lynn glared at Travis. If he knew and did nothing about it, she wouldn't know whom to trust.

"Nay, I knew naught about it. I didn't know he was involved until he and I faced off in the woods when you escaped." Travis absently brushed the bruise on his cheek.

Fin apologized profusely for hitting him. "You came at me like a wild man. I had to get you to calm down somehow so I could explain."

"Why were you with those two in the first place?" Lynn questioned, shaking her head at the two of them. "I don't understand. Why did you help them?"

"I had to. They were my assignment," Fin replied but didn't elaborate any further, leaving Lynn a bit perplexed. She noted the tender way Travis touched Fin's shoulder and he in turn placed his hand on Travis', giving him a look that spoke volumes about their connection. Neither had spoken of their relationship during the tours but she'd sensed a strong, loving bond between them. She cut a glance at Jasper. He watched them intently as if jealous of their outward affection for one another.

"What happened to you at the campsite?" Lynn questioned Travis. She had to know why he wasn't there to help her fight off the intruders.

"I went to refill the canteens and get water for the tea kettle for your morning tea." Travis' brow bunched and he gave Fin a playful glare as he continued. "Someone snuck up behind me and clocked me on the back o' the head, knocking me out cold."

"I had to do it or those two would have beat the shite out o' you." Fin defended his actions.

"I could've taken them," Travis protested, boldly.

"And I would've had to fight you to keep my cover with them. I chose the lesser o' two evils and tried to protect that pretty face o' yours," Fin said, touching Travis' cheek tenderly. "Unfortunately, you gave me no choice in the woods."

Travis nuzzled Fin's hand and kept up the playful pretense of anger, but Lynn read right through it. He wasn't really angry, just teasing Fin. "You gave me a hell o' a headache."

"I'll make it up to you later," Fin replied with a wicked grin that made Lynn blush from the meaning.

"You bet your sweet arse you will," Travis jested lovingly then turned to the ghost, who patiently sat waiting on the rock.

As if that was his cue, Fin moved to sit on the rock in front of him. Travis and Lynn both took seats on available rocks.

"Thank you for taking care o' Lynn," Travis stated sincerely.

"It was the honorable thing to do," Jasper replied sitting taller on the rock. His gaze dropped to Fin as he issued a commanding question. "How be it a MacIntyre be 'n my cave?"

"Your younger sister, Marianna, married Finnies MacIntyre in 1747." He paused as if he waited for Jasper to acknowledge that as fact. When Jasper nodded, he continued. "I am a direct descendant of their union. He was my great-great-great-great grandfather whom I was named after. As such, I am a member o' the society o' clans who came together to protect the fallen MacKinnon brothers."

"I know o' the society." Jasper nodded. "I gave my riddle to Akira, but shared the answer with no one. How be it ye hath found me?"

Lynn noted the genuine look of respect in Fin's eyes. He stared directly at the ghost as he spoke to him as if Jasper sat there in flesh and blood and wasn't really dead.

"From what Grandfather and I have gathered, your sister was a wise woman. She knew o' the oath you took and when you was struck down 'n your prime, gored by a wild boar, she listened to you talking 'n a fevered state before you died. She wrote down every word and prayed it had to do with the location o' the MacKinnon you guarded. You spoke o' a cave and hunting, but gave no sure direction to it." Fin took a breath then nodded toward Travis.

"During our last camping trip, Travis disappeared in a severely inebriated state and somehow ended up here. Not exactly sure how, and he couldn't remember the details, he'd found what I'd been searching years to find." Fin met Travis' stunned look and explained before Travis could ask. "I told you I found you confused and wandering the woods, muttering about a ghost, a cave and a mission. Once you sobered completely, you clammed up and didn't say another word. So I waited, hoping you'd lead me here."

"Why didn't you just ask me? We could've found it together. Instead, you teamed with those two losers over me?" Travis sputtered. Pain showed on his face and Lynn guessed Fin's actions cut him deep.

Fin turned to Travis. Lynn heard the sincerity in his tone as he spoke. "I didn't team with them. I was assigned to keep tabs on them. Unfortunately, those two are descendants o' another clan that swore the oath. But those two don't abide by it. They're out for money and have gone to the dark side."

"The dark side?" Lynn questioned.

"MacGillivray." Jasper and Fin said in unison. Jasper's haunted tone gave the word an eerie ominous sound. Lynn gasped. Travis and Fin each took one of her hands as a show of comfort and support.

Fin nodded as he returned his gaze to Jasper. "There's a descendant o' MacGillivray's on the loose and he's after the Book o' Shadows. From what I've gotten out o' Lonnie and Timothy, he controls some sort o' magical power that scares those two witless. Which isn't hard, considering they don't have a wit between them."

He chuckled and Travis snorted a laugh.

"For centuries, Marianne's information was passed down to the next MacIntyre 'n line with the hope the cure would one day come to save the MacKinnons." Fin stated in a matter-of-fact way, "That day is here, Sire. We don't have much time before MacGillivray's idiots find us. I need to know where the statue is so we can help protect him and quite possibly save him."

Jasper stood. Sadness clearly thickened his words. "Aye. That day is here. Follow me." He floated toward the dimly lit tunnel at the rear of the cave.

When Fin got up, Travis and Lynn did too but Travis gently grabbed Fin's arm turning Fin to face him. "If this is handed down from generation to generation, how is it your Grandfather Ole' Man Thicket knows o' it? He's the only living grandfather I know you have."

Fin grinned. "Thicket is his first name. MacIntyre be his last. Some drunken fool started calling him Ole' Man Thicket years ago and he just never bothered to correct him. After that, everyone used it and his real last name seemed to be forgotten."

Travis laughed, shaking his head. *That* he could believe. Even he never thought it odd that Fin's father's father was called Thicket, when the last name of everyone else in the family was MacIntyre.

They followed Jasper until he led them directly to the frozen MacKinnon brother.

"Lynn hath released him but 'tis only half a freedom. Ye must wait until the fall o' night to begin thy journey," Jasper stated. His words resonated on the cave walls, reinforcing the somberness of his tone.

Lynn knew he wasn't happy this day had come. It meant the man he loved would be leaving him behind. She moved to his side and wished she could hug him without her arms going right through him. Instead, she stood as close as possible even though his coldness chilled her to the bone.

Looking at him, she knew in her heart what he needed to do even if he wasn't sure about doing it. Though it made her hand feel frozen solid, she placed it where his would be if it wasn't transparent and whispered, "You must tell him the way of your heart. It will free your soul."

Frustrated and tired, Lynn sat between Travis and Fin in the late afternoon sun at the mouth of the cave. She was grateful for the provisions Travis had in his pack and was glad he'd even brought stuff from her pack as well. Nibbling on dried fruit and drinking water helped reenergize her system, but did nothing for her spirits. She'd checked on Padon several times knowing he'd still be frozen in his stone casket.

Absently she spoke the anti-curse, not realizing she did. "I wish I knew what the words meant."

"*Step free o' stone. Be ye beast or man. 'Tis love either way. Though ye be mine by night, if not by day.* At least that's what I figure it says." Fin shrugged at Travis' dropped jaw surprised look. "What? I know a bit o' the ol' language."

"I've known you forever and this is the first time you ever told me that one." Travis shook his head. "Just when you think you know someone."

"Didn't think it mattered. Grandma thought it best for the young to know the ways o' the old." Fin grinned as he wagged his eyebrows at Lynn. "And look how it paid off. I helped a lady learn the meaning o' an anti-curse."

"Now don't you be hitting on Lynn," Travis retorted taking a stand between her and Fin.

She couldn't help but laugh at their antics, knowing neither of them was truly interested in her in any physical sense. Fin's green eyes glistened from beneath his mop of unruly black curls. When he took a playful fighting stance to match Travis', his thin frame looked anything but wiry like she'd first thought. He seemed much more leanly muscled but not as tall as Travis. He stood more eye-to-eye with her.

"Okay, gentlemen," she said as she stood and cleared the laughter from her throat. In a playful tone, she teased, "There'll be no fighting over me today. Besides, I know I'm not your flavor."

Travis gently pulled one of her curls as he shot a wink at Fin. "Well maybe you are the one to sway us both. What say you, Fin? You up to a challenge?"

Fin stood in front of Lynn and wrapped his arms around her capturing her between him and Travis. "You are a lot softer and you smell a heck o' a lot better than Travis."

"Hey," Travis jested, feigning being hurt.

Fin released Lynn and immediately took Travis into a hug. "But, I think I like 'em hard and smelling o' the woods and man sweat." He looked back at Lynn. "No offense."

"None taken." Lynn laughed at the two of them lovingly bickering back and forth as they moved to sort the packs and make ready for them to start out the moment the sun went down and Padon came to life.

She settled onto the deerskin blanket taking in the beauty of the world outside the cave. The heavy storm seemed to have washed everything clean giving it a pristine appearance and a fresh scent in the air. Seeing but not really seeing, her thoughts were focused on the task at hand, getting Padon home. She'd told herself repeatedly, that was their first priority, not sex. A slight movement had her turning her head in time to see the rope jiggling. Fin had tied it to one of the large rocks at the mouth of the cave to keep it in place. The end at the top of the cliff was attached tightly to a large tree for when they were ready to climb back up it.

"Umm, guys," she spoke hurriedly and in a hushed tone so whoever was on that rope didn't hear her. "I think we're about to have visitors." She scurried away from the mouth of the cave to stand behind them.

Travis stared at the rope then at Fin. "You think those two found us?"

"It's possible. Didn't think they had any tracking skills 'n 'em." Fin nodded toward the rear of the cave. "Let's wait back there and give them a welcome they'll never forget."

Jasper appeared. "Let me handle this. Ye stay out o' sight." He shot them a devilish grin that displayed how much he loved his job. He disappeared and they knew he hovered near waiting for the opportune moment.

Travis and Fin grabbed their gear, and together with Lynn, hid out of sight in the tunnel. Of course, they only went far enough not to be seen and still watch the action. It seemed like forever before Timothy touched down on the ledge.

"I made it," he yelled up at someone they assumed had to be Lonnie, then he entered the cave. He hadn't taken three steps when Jasper made his appearance. From the looks of it, Timothy didn't see him. That didn't faze Jasper.

Lynn stifled a laugh when Jasper lifted the deerskin blanket from where she'd left it and draped it across Timothy's shoulders. Timothy spun around, his head snapping from side to side.

"Who's there?" he questioned in a panicked voice, snatching the blanket off and tossing it to the side.

Jasper stated boldly and loudly enough it seemed to bounce around the cave. "Ye be trespassing. Stay and be crucified for thy misdeeds or leave and live."

He pelted Timothy with an array of oddities from his collection. A camera hit Timothy in the side of the head. A canteen hard to the gut made Timothy bend at the waist, gasping for air. When Jasper draped the deerskin blanket over his own head and levitated several feet off the ground, Timothy's eyes widened and his feet couldn't move fast enough. He untied the rope from the rock, wrapped it around his waist and tugged on it, screaming, "Pull me up! Pull me up quick!"

When Lonnie didn't react at the proper rate of speed, Timothy started scrambling up the mountainside, taking the rope with him. Rocks tumbled past the opening of the cave as the three in hiding came forward laughing until they cried. They never saw anyone turn so white or move so fast. Jasper floated next to them with a broad smile on his face.

"Did I do that to your satisfaction?"

"You did just fine, Jasper," Travis stated, wiping tears from his eyes.

"Great job," Lynn said the moment she caught her breath.

"Now I understand how you've managed to protect him from being found," Fin declared after clearing his throat. "Unfortunately, all that did was buy us some time. I've got a bad feeling, that's not the last we'll see o' them."

"I'm betting you're right," Travis agreed. He winked at Lynn. "But we've got a way to get him out o' here they don't know about. Fin you said you doubted those two were true believers. Timothy just proved that by not being able to see Jasper. He could only hear him and see the objects Jasper moved."

Fin nodded and Travis continued. "That means, they probably don't know about or care about the anti-curse. So they won't realize the man dressed in the kilt climbing up the mountain is the statue they're looking to cash in on."

"There's a flaw in your theory," Fin stated grimly.

"What?"

"They took the rope. How're we getting to the top?"

"Ye shall leave through the easier way." Jasper spoke the words as if it were a well-known statement to all in the cave. "If ye think Padon and I climbed the side o' the mountain every time to get here, then ye be mistaken. There is an easier path."

Chapter Six

Lynn couldn't believe she stood in front of Padon waiting for the sun to go down so he would step free of his stone prison. Just a little over a week ago, she sat in her bedroom packing for vacation. She hugged herself, not certain if she actually lived in the moment or had been in an accident, hit her head and now lay in a hospital somewhere in Scotland hallucinating she was here.

With her eyes closed tight, she breathed in deep, taking in the cool air of the deepest part of the cave. Never would she have thought this trip would've taken a turn into such an astronomically spiritual encounter, with remarkably unbelievable paranormal activity.

All those years she and Eddie devoured every article and book on ghosts, spirits and paranormal experiences. They'd spent hours researching haunted houses and grounds throughout the state of Texas. They'd saved for the perfect trip to Scotland so they could explore some of the oldest haunts in the world. But Eddie never made it here. It was just her. Still hugging herself, she slowly spun full circle.

Was this real or simply a dream? A wild, outrageous dream...she opened her eyes and focused on the statue...phenomenally handsome, most gorgeous hunk of a man she'd ever seen. She shook off the thought. The main reason she came on this adventure with Travis was to make contact and speak with an otherworldly being.

Which she accomplished.

She'd helped Jasper with his request. She'd spoken the words and Padon was released. Did that mean Jasper would finally tell her how to reach Eddie before he crossed over? Or was this simply the first lesson in a long list of things she needed to know before acquiring the skill to locate Eddie on the other side? So far, every time she attempted to discuss this issue with Jasper, he'd managed to avoid giving her straight answers. Before this was all over, she hoped to wheedle information out of him.

Male voices grew louder, letting her know her time alone with Padon ended. Travis and Fin came down the stairs and moved behind her. Jasper appeared at her side.

"It's time," he spoke. His voice was barely above a whisper yet she heard his distress. If he weren't already dead, the anticipation would probably have killed him.

Lord knows it was killing her. "Nightfall be almost upon us."

Her nerves were taut as a newly strung tennis racquet. She took a deep breath and prayed nothing went wrong. Looking at Jasper and knowing the depth of his love for this man, his pain was her pain.

The ground shook slightly making her take a step for balance. Bright light shot from a growing fissure splitting straight up the center of the statue. Lynn shielded her eyes. Blinking, she tried to see through the cloud of dirt and dust that rose from the disturbance. She fanned the air in front of her face, attempting to clear it enough to focus. Though the whole incident happened in a flash, it felt longer to Lynn before she saw Padon.

Bits and pieces of stone lay scattered on the ground around his bare feet. Padon stood as if ready to pounce. A layer of dust covered his kilt and flesh as her gaze slid upward. It surprised her to see his sword held poised and pointed, unwavering at Travis and Fin, keeping them at bay. It appeared as if he dared either of them to move. From the looks of it, neither of them did. She couldn't be certain if they even took a full breath.

The massive size of Padon's arms left no doubts about his ability to wield lethal damage with the ancient instrument of death. Following the line of those tightly coiled muscles led her gaze to his shoulders and his chest, which heaved with each intake and exhale of air. He breathed heavily. Was he scared or in shock from the transformation?

Though she already knew his body, she stood soaking him in for a few seconds giving him time to re-acclimate with his surroundings. He appeared distraught and confused. Did the curse make him that way? Did he remember her or had their rendezvous in the waterfall been wiped from his memory when he fell to the curse for the night?

She couldn't help but note his square jawline was held so tight a faint twitch started in his cheek beneath his left eye. He had the sexiest set of blue-green eyes even though his stare was so intense, never leaving either of the men as if waiting for them to make the first move. Lynn sensed Padon hadn't noticed she was there. A raw intensity wafted off him keeping *her* completely aware of him.

Would he actually hurt Travis or Fin? She couldn't let that happen. Lynn stepped forward and touched his arm, garnering his attention. Padon turned his eyes toward her and his gaze softened with recognition. But he didn't relax.

"My wee one." His voice sounded hoarse as he spoke and she wished she had a drink for him to soothe his throat. "I woke and was startled by the presence o' two unknowns. Are ye safe or do ye need me to dispatch these adversaries from this place?" She had no doubt of whom he spoke because he didn't lower his sword simply flicked it causing her gaze to follow the direction to which it pointed. Travis and Fin stood stock still, waiting for Padon to drop his weapon.

Jasper laughed heartily as he appeared beside Travis and Fin. "Nay, *m'cariad*. These men be here to help. Meet Travis Shain and my kinfolk, Fin MacIntyre."

"Ye kinfolk?" Padon questioned. His eyebrow arched as he lowered his sword.

Jasper quickly explained everything to Padon in their native tongue of Gaelic. Lynn listened in awe of the beauty of the language and wished she understood. From the expression on Padon's face, it was clear Jasper spoke of Fin explaining how they were related and why the two men were here.

When he woke, Padon's vision was not clear and for an instant he knew not where he was. Two men stood in his line-of-sight, strangely dressed but it seemed they were unarmed. But he took no chances and kept them at swords length until he regained composure. Where had they come from and were they associated with MacGillivray had been the questions that filtered through his fogged brain. His heavy headedness felt as if he drank a vat of ale and the cobwebs lingered across his eyes blurring his vision.

Though he'd had a lot of time to think while trapped throughout the day, Padon's thoughts were contorted, making it difficult to sort out time and place for several long seconds. *Cursed.* That's what Lynn and Jasper told him last night. His *brathairs* and he were cursed to stone for centuries by the black magic words spoken from MacGillivray.

Lynn's touch to his arm grounded him and warmed his cold heart. Her smile eased his angst and had him wanting to protect her, hold her and kiss her until his world was made right. Jasper's laughter had interrupted the moment. He listened to Jasper's explanation of who the two men were and why they were there. By the time Jasper was finished, Padon needed a second.

To gain his bearings, he closed his eyes. Though he tried not to let it, the last memory from that fateful day roared to life, taking over his mind making him relive it again as it had throughout the hours trapped in his stone tomb. He heard his *brathair* Ian yell some sort of warning then silence. No longer hearing Ian's voice, he'd grabbed his sword and left his room in search of what happened. The sight of his *brathair* frozen in stone terrified him. What sort of black magic was this? He heard a noise and tracked it.

MacGillivray stood in the great hall, circling his *brathair* Struan, who now resembled poor Ian. Frozen, unable to move nor fight. Padon sprang into the room, sword held ready to spear MacGillivray through his darkened heart. The bastard turned as Padon ran towards him. He didn't blink just spoke a verse and life stood still. The last he remembered. His sword stopped mere inches from the demon's chest. Somehow he knew before his brain shut down he'd fallen to the same fate as his *brathairs*.

When he rose from the curse for the first time last night, he thought it was a bad dream. That it hadn't really happened, because he woke in the hunting cave and not the castle. He'd shaken it off as a horrible nightmare brought on by too much drink. Seeing a woman in the waterfall gave him an opportunity to believe his theory. She was beautiful and receptive and a gift given to him by his best friend, Jasper. At least that's what he'd tried to convince himself as they'd shared intimacies. The appearance of Jasper's ghost had set him straight with the help of Lynn.

Padon opened his eyes and let his gaze glide across Lynn's angelic features. Her nearness aroused his desire and made it easier for him to shove the nightmare into a corner of his mind, for now.

Knowing a descendent of MacGillivray's lived to carry on his demonic work shredded his soul. He gallantly swallowed his hatred and held it deep within, waiting for the perfect time to let it resurface into a useful tool of revenge. No one need know this level of anger he kept at bay, especially this gentle lamb beside him. Her beauty knew no such beast like the one he knew would rear its ugly head once he found MacGillivray.

"Padon, are you all right?" she asked.

"Aye, my wee one." He liked her soft voice and its odd lilt turned him on. A Texas twange she had called it. He knew not where she was from, but admired how they grew their women—full-figured, with ample bosom and a bottom strong enough to handle childbirth. Aye, she was built nicely. "Just gaining my bearings. Takes a moment to shake the curse from my bones. Having ye beside me makes it an easier task to accomplish." He lifted her hand to his lips and pressed a kiss to her knuckles.

Blue eyes filled with the brightness of the sun held a hint of joy and happiness within them as heat colored her cheeks. When she smiled, it lit her angelic features and he sensed she truly understood his needs. He fingered the soft auburn curls that framed her face. It was cut too short for his liking. If he asked, would she grow it long for him?

Would she get mad if he tugged one straight and let it go? Before he could stop himself, his hand took action. Looping a curl between his fingers, he gently pulled it straight and let go. It did exactly as he thought it would by popping right back into a tight curl beside her face. She didn't slap his hand away. Instead she laughed. The warmth of her laughter filled him making him smile.

"The only time those aren't so curly is when I let it grow long," Lynn stated, fingering her hair as if assuring it had returned to its proper place.

He touched her chin with the tip of his finger, lifting her face to look into her eyes, again. "Long. Aye. Would be nice on ye, my wee one."

Padon stared at her until the realization of what Jasper had said sunk in. These men were here to help him return to Castle MacKinnon. Though he hated looking away from those gorgeous eyes, he dropped his hand to his side and looked at Jasper across Lynn's head. "Man by night. Stone by day. Apparently that part o' the anti-curse be true."

"Aye," Jasper replied.

"Castle MacKinnon cannot be reached 'n one night."

Fin stepped forward and offered, "We have a way to get you home. We just have to get to my grandfather's farm before sunrise."

"How far?" Padon asked looking at the wiry man.

"Travis and I have made the hike 'n a day and a half, but that was pushing it." Fin looked him directly in the eye. Padon liked that. It was a true measure of a man. If he couldn't or wouldn't meet your gaze then he was untrustworthy.

Padon grabbed the sheath that held his sword. "We shall leave now."

"We'll gather our gear."

"Return here, quickly," Jasper called to the retreating backs of Travis and Fin as they hustled toward the stairs.

"Do you have shoes or a shirt for him?" She poised the question to Jasper. Lynn's sweet concern for his state of undress made him pause as he slipped the sheath around him.

Padon grinned at her. "Milady, 'tis not a concern."

Jasper laughed heartily. "Lynn. Padon tends to be without shoes and shall we say clothes as much as propriety allows. Ye be lucky he had on a kilt the day he was cursed." At the mention of that day, a dark shadow seemed to pass over Jasper's expression. "Thy curse be o' no luck at all. If'n I were there I could have saved ye."

"Nay, Jasper," Padon replied in a reassuring tone. "MacGillivray was hell bent on ending Clan MacKinnon. Ye would only have fallen to the curse as well."

"I should never have left the castle that night," Jasper snapped but more at himself rather than at Padon.

Padon rubbed his chin and his tone was one laced with innuendo. "As I recall it, ye left with a young maiden."

"Aye." Jasper's head hung low in shame.

"Did ye enjoy the night?"

"Nay," Jasper admitted. "Naught happened. I tried and failed. She was not to my liking."

Padon laughed. "More likely the amount o' ale we drank that night interfered."

Jasper let loose a nervous laugh but Lynn saw right through it. Padon didn't seem to be catching on to what Jasper was trying to say. When Jasper looked at her, his expression spoke what he couldn't and Lynn's heart took a nosedive to her stomach. From what she understood, Jasper felt guilty for not being at the castle to save his friend. And worst of all, he was trying to prove himself to be a man by bedding a woman, which apparently didn't work. Oh Lord, what could she do to help him?

Padon moved toward the waterfall. She followed. Jasper lingered where Padon had stood for centuries. When she looked back, she saw a light brighten around him and he shook his head as if saying no to someone she could not see.

"Padon," Lynn called out and he stopped. She pointed to Jasper.

His shape flickered and it appeared he struggled to keep his visceral appearance. Padon hurried to his side. He knelt in front of his friend. Tears shimmered in his eyes.

"'Tis time for ye to go?" His voice cracked and Lynn sensed he felt deeply for Jasper.

"Aye. The Angels call. Ye are free. My presence be no longer needed." Jasper looked at Lynn. His eyes seemed darkened and filled with sadness. "Take care o' him. See him home safely for me."

She stepped forward reaching in the direction of Jasper's cheek. It didn't matter her fingertips sunk into his image and coldness shot along her arm. "Tell him," she simply stated as she held his heartbroken stare. When he shook his head, she said it again. "Tell him. Leave this world in peace and your heart free. Don't let regret darken your heavenly travels."

Jasper looked as if he wanted to protest but changed his mind. He floated to kneel before Padon and took his face in his hands. Lynn swallowed against the sudden lump in her throat at the beauty of what happened in front of her. If Padon felt the chill she knew graced his skin from Jasper's touch, he didn't show it.

"I hath loved ye my whole life and more," Jasper said. Passion and love filled each word of his declaration and Lynn had to breathe deeply to keep from crying.

"And I hath loved ye as close as one o' my *brathairs*," Padon answered. His rich baritone seemed to falter as he spoke.

"I know my *gaol* – love, *m'caraid* – my friend," Jasper continued. His fingers on one hand disappeared when he ran them through Padon's hair, yet the hair didn't move from the touch. "I hath been thy bloodless *brathair*. In my heart, ye hath been my *leannan* – lover." Jasper rose. His image became less visible by the second.

Padon leapt to his feet reaching for Jasper, but his hands swept through his ghostly frame. "I knew, Jasper," Padon admitted, raw emotion laced his words. "I knew. But I did not feel thy same kind o' *gaol* for ye." His head hung low. "Please forgive me."

Jasper's hand cupped Padon's chin and though Lynn knew he felt nothing but cold, Padon lifted his face to meet Jasper's gaze. "There be nothing to forgive. We shared a friendship like no other." Jasper smiled. "I am free to walk 'n the Garden o' Angels. Ye are free to follow thy heart, my *gaol*."

He leaned and brushed a kiss across Padon's lips and Lynn could no longer hold back her tears. The look in Padon's eyes said it all. He loved Jasper and that was a memory Jasper would take with him to the other side.

Jasper floated until he was near the ceiling then he spun at a rapid rate of speed. Padon placed a fist across his heart and stared directly at Jasper. "Thank ye, *m'caraid*. May ye rest 'n peace. Ye deserved so much more than me."

"Nay," came Jasper's voice from the spinning ball of light. "Ye were *m'caraid* and that was enough for me."

Jasper suddenly stopped spinning. He shot Padon a smile then burst into a flash of brilliant colors and stars, which rained down upon them. His spirit was gone.

Chapter Seven

She couldn't be sure how much they heard or saw, but the spell of the scene that had just played out before her was broken when either Travis or Fin cleared his throat loudly. Padon swiped the back of his hand across his eyes, and she knew he hid his tears from the men. But if he'd looked at them like she did, he would have seen them both brushing tears from their eyes as well. They understood the love between men.

"We must leave," Padon stated then turned and headed for the waterfall again.

No one questioned his direction. He walked along the ledge that ran toward the waterfall. He glanced over his shoulder at them. Lynn followed close behind him with Travis behind her and Fin behind him. At the waterfall, he gave them a nod then disappeared into the cascading water. Lynn paused for a second not certain if he remembered the way correctly. She'd had sex with Padon in the waterfall, but hadn't noticed a pathway behind it. She looked at Travis and shrugged but wasn't given a chance to say anything. A strong hand reached from the water, grabbed her hand, tugged her into the steady stream of water and through to the other side.

The wet stones made her slip and she fell against his slick body. His arm held her securely around the waist. Water dripped from his hair giving him a playful, yet sexy roguish appeal. When his gaze met hers, moist heat formed low in her pelvis. Lordy, he had a way of turning her on with simply a look filled with sexual innuendo. His eyes seemed to darken and his muscles flinched tighter around her. He was about to kiss her and every ounce of her wanted him too as she pursed her lips making ready for his touch.

Travis and Fin pushed through the waterfall to stand behind her. Lynn gathered her wits and pressed her palm flat against his healthy chest and steadied herself before easing out of the safety of his hold.

"Thank you," she managed to push from her suddenly dry lips. If they hadn't been interrupted, she would've gotten another taste of his magnificent mouth.

He simply nodded and turned without a word, letting her know he was a bit out of sorts by the intrusion as well. His gorgeous back of wet, slick muscles disappeared into an opening in the wall behind the waterfall she hadn't noticed while washing and having sex. Well, the sex part had kept her a bit preoccupied to the point she wouldn't have noticed if a train had barreled out of that tunnel. Travis nudged her arm with a flashlight from his pack.

"Here, you might need this."

Lynn nodded. "Thank you. I forgot to ask if you wanted me to carry anything."

"Nay," Travis replied. "You worry about keeping up with him and let me and Fin do the hauling this time."

She switched on the light and entered the mouth of the tunnel. She located Padon standing at a fork in the extended cave. He held an ancient looking lantern in his hand and appeared to be trying to light it when he looked her way. His brows bunched and he dropped the object. When she reached him, he pointed at her hand.

"Magic?"

"No," Lynn replied, realizing he wouldn't know anything about the gadgets of her time. She took a second to explain as she handed it to him. "It's a flashlight. You turn it on and off with this switch." She placed it in his hand, put her hand over his and maneuvered his fingers on the switch showing him how it worked. He played with it several times before finally leaving it on.

He grinned at her and his expression was that of a bewildered kid with a new toy. "This way," he said with an edge of excitement in his voice that had her smiling inwardly as he walked into the left corridor.

She followed as did Travis and Fin. It seemed like hours they travelled this route at a steady pace, which wouldn't have been possible if Padon hadn't taken a hold of her hand to help guide her through the rough terrain. At times, Travis was so close behind her, she swore she felt his breath on her neck. Was he claustrophobic and scared? She shrugged off the thought and figured it was just so they wouldn't get separated.

The moon was high in the sky when they reached the other end of the tunnel. Moonbeams shone down in an array of streaks of nightshade grays and whites where she stood looking at the opening in the earth's floor. Padon handed her the flashlight, grasped her hand and pointed the beam at a makeshift stairwell made from rocks and boulders. It was definitely man-made, but looked as if it hadn't been used in many years.

He moved to the stairwell and tested the first few steps then carefully one by one ascended them. At the top, he stuck his head through the opening. His arms went above his head and he seemed to hoist himself out with ease. After several seconds, his head poked through the hole and he motioned for Lynn to follow.

Not certain about the stairs, she decided if they held a man Padon's size then she shouldn't be a problem. At the top, she shone the light accidentally into his eyes and he winced.

"Sorry," she said.

"Give me your hands."

She turned off the light and tucked it in her shirt between her breasts so she wouldn't lose it then did as instructed. With both hands held over her head, Padon grabbed hold of her forearms and she clasped her hands tight as possible around his. Smoothly, he lifted her free of the opening. He set her on the ground beside him then leaned in to help the next person. She moved out of the way. She couldn't go far. A wall of stone stood behind her. Across from the hole was a thickly woven semi-circle of boulders, trees and underbrush. She wasn't exactly sure how they would exit.

With the last man out, Padon turned to the next task. He scaled one of the boulders close to the wall of rock, using the wall for leverage as he climbed. Once on top, he laid flat and it appeared as if he scouted their surroundings before signaling it was clear to climb. He'd made it look so easy, Lynn figured she'd give it her best shot.

Travis and Fin were behind her in case she slipped. Near the top, Padon reached over and hoisted her the rest of the way. Going down the other side was easy. Padon jumped and landed on his feet then turned and held his hands out motioning it was her turn. Lynn took a breath and a leap of faith that he'd catch her and landed in his arms. He didn't even make an oaf sound like she thought he would by catching a full-figured gal like herself.

Her breasts brushed against his chest making her nipples react. Between the damp shirt from the waterfall and being pressed against his naked chest and abdomen, she was on fire for him. This wasn't normally like her. Lynn Woodberry didn't act like a hormone-driven wild woman over anyone, but Padon wasn't a simple anyone. She looked at the rugged face of the man whose arms held her and tightened her grip around his neck. Lord help her, the thoughts singeing her brain right now would surely get her sent directly to hell, do not pass go, do not collect two hundred dollars.

She did her best to sound calm when she said on a strained whisper, "You can put me down now."

Instead he held her closer, turned and walked a few feet away before sliding her down the length of him to stand on her feet. He made sure she had her balance before he let go. Now if she could only breathe. That man stole the air from her lungs with a single touch. Being in his arms, she felt like a tiny doll. It didn't even look as if he strained a muscle when he caught her or carried her. Lynn liked that. She smiled at him.

He leaned toward her and her mouth dried. Her eyes locked on his sensual lips, that sexy cleft in his chin she wanted to taste with the tip of her tongue. Instead of kissing her, he tugged the flashlight from where it stuck out from between her breasts. He flicked it on and gave her a drop-dead sexy smile. She was thankful it was dark enough he couldn't see her blush. That was twice now she'd hungered for his kiss and not gotten one. Damn, this was going to be a long night.

Lynn watched his muscles flex as he helped Travis and Fin. With every move he made, she had no doubt Padon somehow had visited her in her dream the first night in the woods. He moved the same way her dream man did when he'd saved her from the cliff. Strong and effortless. She wasn't sure how it happened but she was damn sure it was him. Lynn tried to redirect her thoughts from kissing Padon. When it hit her, she'd never gotten any straight answers out of Jasper.

Now the opportunity was lost forever. Lynn didn't get the chance to think it through. Padon grabbed her hand and they were cutting through the woods in the dead of night. He didn't trip or stumble and it looked as if being without shoes was as natural for him as wearing boots was for her. Lynn had to concentrate to keep up, especially in the dark. Though the moon was high and they had flashlights it was still treacherous to her. The men didn't seem to be having any problem. Then again, they'd camped in these woods many times and had to know the terrain pretty well.

Besides, they didn't have a sexy man holding their hands dragging them through the forest causing them inner turmoil like what was happening to her. His touch was making her insides haywire with needs she thought were buried with Eddie. It didn't help when she stumbled and his fast reflexes kept her from falling. Those big hands made her hot to the point if she wouldn't look like a bumbling fool she'd keep tripping over stuff just to have him catch her.

Lynn rolled her eyes at the thought. Now wasn't the time for her hormones to finally remember they existed and kick into high gear. It was hard to control since she'd already experienced a wonderful bout of sex in his arms. Her brain seemed to only focus on that with every brush of his body to hers as they wound their way through the woods. She knew they had to cover as much ground as possible before daybreak, find a place to hide and hope Lonnie and Timothy weren't bright enough to track them.

Breathe, Lynn, breathe, she told herself. Think of nothing but getting out of here. Looking at the way the moonlight skimmed across his naked back made that almost impossible as she followed him closely.

Padon knew this trail well, but time had hidden it from lack of use. The growth of trees and underbrush caused him to redirect their path. He managed to use the stars to help guide them in the right direction. Many times, he and Jasper made the trek to the cave while hunting. The ravine was a menagerie of wild game upon which to feast. They'd taken what they needed for their families and left the rest to grow bigger for next time. He never imagined the cave would become his home for centuries. It hurt his heart to know how Jasper felt and why he'd traded a peaceful rest in the Garden of Angels to watch over and protect him. It was a debt he knew not how to repay.

Aye. He loved Jasper but not in the same manner. He'd suspected for years Jasper was different. Hell, he knew in his heart how Jasper felt, but simply accepted it without acting on it. Sex with another man did not appeal to him. He chanced a look over his shoulder. Though sex with a certain curly-headed, robust woman named Lynn wouldn't be something he'd turn down if offered again.

A smile tugged at his lips as the memory of the soft sensation of her hair twisting in his fingers felt right before he released it to spring back against her face. *Och*, what a beautiful face she had, round in shape, with bright blue eyes, a cute little nose and a set of full lips he hungered to taste over and over. Sweet. She tasted sweeter than any berry he'd scavenged in the woods.

He knew the sweetness of her lips was great. It set his imagination on fire wondering about the flavor and exquisite taste of the nectar from her treasure to the point his mouth watered in anticipation. He did not know why she wore men's trews but liked the way they fit her pleasantly shaped bottom. A woman with a solid foundation always piqued his sexual interest and Lynn was solidly perfect for him. A big lunk like himself needed a healthy woman to satisfy his needs. He'd never touched a skin and bones lass. That sort never sparked his lust. Nay, what he needed held his hand and hurried along behind him. He knew she could handle him and that knowledge made him hard between his thighs.

Though he tried to stop the flow of thoughts about sex and Lynn, he couldn't. The image of her breasts popped into his head sending the blood straight to his bawls. Her loose top did nothing to hide the sizable breasts he'd enjoy spending hours tending to, if she let him hold them in his hands again. When he tugged the flashlight from between them, it was a chore not to slip his hand in and caress those luscious tender mounds. His mouth hungered with want for her nipples. Ahh, he wanted desperately to suckle what he knew was perfectly proportioned to the rest of her beautiful body and sized just right for him.

For the first time all night, he tripped. He righted himself before he fell but not quickly enough to keep Lynn from bumping into his backside. Her breasts pressed into his back. One on either side of his sword. Her hand came palm flat to the bare skin at his waist and the warmth of her touch added to his growing desire to sample all of her attributes, repeatedly. Her breath skittered across his flesh. His shaft reacted instantly making him glad it was the dead of night and she was behind him and couldn't see the prominent bulge occurring in his kilt.

Not being able to control his instant reaction to her had to be a side effect of being imprisoned for so long. Many times in his youth, he'd woken horny, but never this badly. Uncontrollable lust grew from the pit of his bawls and spread warmth and need to every inch of him. Inwardly he shivered against the rush of heat thickening his blood and his shaft.

"You okay?" Her question came on a heavy breath and he knew he'd pushed her too fast in the dark.

He breathed deep for a second trying to will himself to calm before he faced her. Cupping her chin, he replied, "Aye. Do ye be 'n need o' a break, wee one?"

"No, I can manage."

Her words claimed one thing, but her actions spoke another. Padon knew she was tired but wouldn't admit it. Stubborn. Willing to continue even though her body begged for a rest. Her shoulders sagged. The exhausted sound in her heavy breathing let him know she struggled to maintain the pace he'd set. He liked her willingness to continue even though she seemed worn thin.

Och, he wished she breathed heavily for another reason that he induced. Padon gently brushed his thumb across her lip. It seemed to beckon to be kissed yet he fought the urge. They were not alone. Pulling his gaze from hers and dropping his hand to his side, he stared at the sky trying to determine the hour and their location in reference to the stars. They'd made decent time in their travels but daylight would be upon them long before they reached Fin's grandfather's farm. Making a decision he knew would torment his already hardened condition, Padon maneuvered his sheathed sword to hang across his chest, then turned and squatted in front of Lynn.

Looking over his shoulder at her, he said, "Lass. Ye are tired and we've a long path to follow. Please let me be the horse to carry ye whilst ye rest."

"I—" she stuttered as if searching for the right way to say something. "I'm too heavy for you to carry. I'll be fine."

He laughed lightly then clasped her behind the knees and pulled her closer. "Milady, ye weight be o' no factor to me. Now, let's not waste time. Hop on let's be off."

He tugged at her knees and was happy she did what he wanted. When she had a good hold around his neck, he lifted to his feet with her legs wrapped around his waist. Damn, the heat of her felt good against the small of his back. Padon swallowed and prayed for the strength to ignore the things her closeness was doing to him. They had to make good time and this was simply the best way to continue. At least that's what he tried to convince himself though in the back of his mind, he really liked the brush of the apex between her thighs against him with every step. And with those breasts pressed tight to his flesh, his imagination took off like a hawk in flight after prey.

Why hadn't he thought to carry her against his chest instead of on his back? She'd probably fit perfectly and bounce sensually against his shaft in tune with his gait. Padon admonished the thought and tried desperately to think of anything but sex. With Lynn on his back, that wasn't happening. Each step was a task in self-control but did nothing to cool the desire pumping from his bawls to his shaft.

This was going to be a long, long trek through the woods.

Lynn snuggled against him. His warmth was a welcomed cloak that cut some of the night air chill. His scent filled her nose. Woodsy. Masculine. Umm. He smelled delicious. His muscles bunched beneath her and brushed her rhythmically as he moved smoothly along the trail that only he could see. If Travis and Fin were not behind them, she knew she would've kissed him when they'd stopped.

He'd tripped. She was sure of it, but he claimed he was okay. Was he not telling the truth? He didn't seem like the type to lie. Was he just as tired as she? From the way he moved, sure-footedly and with the grace of a wild animal native to these woods, she got the impression he could go all night. Her eyes widened at the idea of marathon sex with Padon. Oh Lordy, where had that come from?

From the over sensitive bud hidden in the folds of flesh between your thighs that at this moment loved the constant bump against this hunk's back, that's where. The naughty voice at the back of her brain nearly shouted out loud. Lynn closed her eyes. Her nipples were pointed from the jostle in his walk, causing them to move up and down along his taut muscles, they ached and hurt. The strap of his sword's sheath added to the friction and for a split second the image of her hands bound above her head with the length of leather shot behind her closed lids.

Bondage. She'd never even considered it. Was Padon into it? God, what was she thinking? It had to be a mind trick played on her senses from the significant amount of tiredness knotting her limbs. She normally didn't think like this, like a horn-dog in need of a good lay.

Padon picked up his pace when they reached an open area. He ran across. His hands moved from her knees to cup her ass, lifting her higher on his back. Her mound rubbed the buckle of the strap of the sheath. The faster he ran, the harder she bounced. His fingers kneaded her bottom and if they followed the curve inward just a little bit more, he'd realize just how wet he'd gotten her without even trying.

The moment he reached the cover of the woods, he stopped. Moonlight shone on his face as he looked over his shoulder at her. Their gazes locked on one another. Lynn's heart pounded as if she'd been the one doing the sprint across the field. Padon stretched and she followed suit. Ever so lightly, their lips touched at an odd angle for a moment but it was enough.

Travis and Fin burst from the field into the woods at a gallop startling Lynn, who jerked from the kiss.

"Man," Travis gasped as he wheezed in and out, "for an old guy, you're fast."

"Aye, when need be. But I no be fast at everything," he stated with a sly wink at Lynn, who hid her smile in his hair. On a low whisper meant only for her, he added, "There be things 'n life that need be savored slow."

He readjusted her on his back, keeping his hands firmly planted beneath her bum with his palms open giving her the perfect seat. Now if he'd just keep those damn thick thumbs of his still, she could probably think of something other than sex, but she doubted it. Slow, sensual circles near her anus kept her body humming with need. From the look he'd shot her over his shoulder right before their lips touched, she knew he knew exactly what he did to her.

Now the trick was, how would they get out of these woods, find a place to hide and somehow steal some alone time before the sun hit the sky. If nothing else, she wanted to taste those sexy lips of his.

Chapter Eight

It was just before daybreak when they finally stopped. They were running out of time and it became evident they weren't going to make it out of the woods by first light. It had taken them longer than anticipated. Fin led them to an old hunting shack located on the farthest outreaches of his grandfather's land. His father and grandfather built the shack but hadn't used it in years. Fin and Travis tended to follow the game deeper into the woods and camped when they hunted. Even though it leaned to the left and a tree was the only thing keeping it from falling over, it would have to do for shelter for Padon.

Fin opened the door to the one room wooden abode. "Travis and I shall take turns keeping watch for those two. But I doubt they've got the balls to come after us."

Travis clapped Fin on the back. "You rest first once we set up the tents. I've got this watch."

"The shack is yours." Fin nodded toward Padon. "It may be good to keep you out o' sight. We'll set up the tents back 'n the woods a ways from here so if'n those two do stumble upon us, they'll find that camp first."

He nodded to Travis and they turned to walk back into the woods.

Now that they were at a point to rest, Lynn was glad they'd taken a few minutes to gather the pup tents from their campsite when they'd come upon it. Earlier, she'd been scared the stop gave Lonnie and Timothy a chance to catch up. Travis and Fin had been quick about gathering what they needed and they'd moved on in a rather timely fashion. Fin's opinion on it was that without the visual signs of the campsite where they'd taken Lynn, those two wouldn't be able to determine if they were headed back in the right direction or not.

"Aye," Padon stated as he released Lynn.

Her arms ached from circling his neck for hours. His hands may have made a fine seat but she'd still clung to him to help keep from falling. The imprint of his hands lingered on her butt and she swore she still felt the tiny swirls of his thumbs. She closed her eyes. How did he do that the whole time? Didn't his fingers get tired? The sensitive area between her ass cheeks was glad he didn't. She liked the way he kept her on edge, sliding his thumbs close to but not touching her anus. She'd wanted him to slip them more inward caressing along her slit until he reached her clit and soothed the rising pressure bringing her relief. It throbbed to the point just sliding off him nearly made her come.

Not wanting him to see how much he affected her, Lynn walked on shaky legs into the shack. Two old cots lined opposite walls. A rickety-looking wooden table with two matching chairs sat in the middle of the room. On the far wall hung a rusted cabinet. Both doors were open showing nothing was in it. A potbelly stove sat in the corner directly across from the corner touching the tree. It was probably the only other thing helping keep the shack upright with its solid-looking stovepipe angled through the ceiling.

Warm hands slid around her waist from behind, startling her at first. He tugged her close and she couldn't miss the hardness beneath his kilt pressing against her bottom. It pleased her to know he was in the same needy condition as she. She liked the feel of him wrapped around her, holding her, but there was something she really wanted and time was running out. Lynn turned in his arms.

She didn't have to ask. It seemed he wanted the same. Padon leaned, pulling her up in his arms, bringing her onto her toes. Lips touched lips in a kiss she never wanted to end. Soft and tender quickly became passion-filled need. Each giving and taking, communicating their desire for one another through this kiss. Tongue caressed tongue in a sensual dance, increasing her hunger for this man.

His hands slid down her back to cup her ass, holding her tighter against his hard-on. Damn, he felt great. Even though her hips ached from having her legs wrapped around his waist for most of the night, she desperately wanted to hop back on except this time she wanted to ride his front and not his back. One hand left her rear and slid between them to caress her through her jeans. Thick fingers rubbed firmly in just the right spot. The pressure in her grew even more, but it didn't take much before it released, bursting like an overstressed dam. Moisture soaked her panties. She broke free of their kiss, gasping and flushed, not believing he'd done that to her without making skin-to-skin contact.

She dropped her gaze to the floor unable to look at him. This wasn't like her to act like such a loose woman, but he seemed to bring out the pure sex-driven side of her nature. His finger eased beneath her chin and gently forced her to lift her head, but she kept her eyes closed. She wasn't ready to explain herself. She had no explanation other than he made her so excited she couldn't control herself in his presence. Padon didn't give her a chance to retreat into herself.

He brushed a kiss across her lips. "I told ye before, there be no shame 'n this, Lynn." He kissed one closed eyelid then the other. "'Tis natural to want to be 'n another's arms."

Padon captured her mouth in a tender kiss she was helpless to resist. His lips demanded she return their favor. His tongue caressed hers into reacting. Lynn was lost in his arms not wanting him to stop, but he did. When he pulled away, she was breathless as was he, which made her smile. It seemed the overwhelming sexual effect was mutual.

He lowered to her ear. In his rich baritone, he simply stated something that touched her and sent a thrill straight to her core. "There be some things 'n life that need be savored slowly. Ye be one o' those treasures. I failed to realize that at our first coupling. Be advised." He grinned wickedly. "Our next shall be a savoring o' ye attributes, my wee one until we both be sated."

Lynn shivered from his honest admission as desire flowed through her. This man had her hot and ready, but they were out of time. Electricity sizzled in the air and her heart skipped a beat. She held her breath hoping against hope the curse wouldn't happen.

He stepped back placing a wide gap between them as the first rays of sunshine snuck in through the windows, open door and cracks in the walls. Right before the curse took him, he met her gaze with one filled with lust and sexual promise.

"Be safe 'til next we meet at the fall o' night, my wee one."

Lynn watched in awe as the curse engulfed him in a casket of stone. He stood arrow straight, hands held together in front of his kilt and she noted he'd moved his sword into its proper position on his back. She circled his frozen figure and was simply amazed at the powerful magic that occurred before her eyes. Dragging her fingertips along his body as she walked, she sensed he rested within this unwanted cocoon but knew he wasn't at peace.

He wouldn't be until the curse was broken and the MacGillivray descendant had taken his last breath. Lynn leaned against his chest, pressing her cheek and ear to the area where his heart should be. Did he breathe while entombed? Was he conscious?

She swore she heard his heartbeat, low and faint deep within the solid wall around him. A single tear slid down her cheek as she straightened looking into those lifeless eyes that earlier held such heat and desire. She couldn't imagine how awful it must be to be locked away for so many years only to be partially freed. He'd experienced two nights of freedom only to be turned back into a stone statue with the rise of the sun.

Half a freedom.

The words echoed in her ears. His sister Akira was right. This was half a freedom. No man deserved to live like this, ever. Lynn plopped onto one of the chairs and hoped it held her weight. If it took everything she had, she planned to help release Padon completely from this curse.

No matter what it took.

After staring idly at him for several long minutes, Lynn got up and closed the door. She set the rusty latch in place and shoved a chair underneath the knob as an added measure of protection. From the looks of it, a good brisk wind would undo the door without much of a challenge. She tugged the old curtains closed hoping to keep unwanted onlookers from peeping in and catching sight of Padon. If Lonnie and Timothy got past Travis and Fin, she didn't want to make it easy to find Padon. Not going to happen on her watch. She was the second line of defense.

Lynn noted a thick stick lay on the floor beneath each window. Picking one up, she secured it between the top of the window and the upper edge of the windowsill as an added measure to help the lock hold shut. She repeated the process on the other window and felt a smidgeon more secure in her surroundings.

Beating one of the cots with the broom she found in the corner, she dusted it off and lay down. It wasn't much for comfort but it would do. She rolled onto her side facing Padon so she could keep an eye on him. Full sun on the shack warmed the inside to a cozy temperature making her sleepier. Unable to fight it, her eyes grew heavy and exhaustion seeped through her commanding that she rest.

* * * * *

Travis and Fin worked together to quickly set up the makeshift camp several yards away from the shack. They wanted to remain within earshot in case Lynn needed them, but they didn't want it visible from their site. Thankfully, the trees shielded the shack from direct view. They knew where it was, but for the untrained eye, it didn't stand out and would go overlooked.

"You know, " Travis said as he tossed his gear into one of the tents. "It just struck me, why did you kidnap Lynn? She didn't know where to find the cave. Why not take me, instead?"

"She was easier. At least that was the idea. Who knew the lass would put up such a fight?" Fin grinned then shook his head. "It was Lonnie's idea. He thought she would make fine bait to get you to cooperate 'n finding the cave."

"Guess he never realized he already had the perfect bait for me while he had you in his midst," Travis quipped then kissed Fin long and hard. When they separated, Travis kept Fin in his arms and arched his eyebrow. "I'm confused. How did he know about the cave 'n the first place. Did you tell him?"

"Nay. He was in the pub when you told Lynn the tale about your night 'n the woods."

"How 'n the hell did he overhear that?" Travis knew he'd kept his voice low and had made sure no one was close when he told her.

Fin stepped from the hug and returned to setting up camp as he spoke. "You know those stupid gadgets that claim to increase hearing so you can listen in on someone else's conversation without them knowing?" When Travis nodded, Fin continued. "Apparently, they work. He had one 'n his ear as he sat at the bar behind you and focused on your conversation."

Travis' jaw dropped. He was at a loss, not believing something he'd seen in the *Odd Gadgets and Gizmos* magazine actually worked. Worse yet, an idiot like Lonnie had used it and listened in on his conversation with Lynn.

"Why me? How'd he know I knew anything about where a MacKinnon was hidden?"

"He didn't," Fin replied. "He got that thing that day 'n the mail and decided to try it out. You just happened to be 'n the wrong place at the wrong time. I'd already been given the assignment to keep an eye on them and knew they liked to hang 'n that particular pub. It just worked out we also led our groups there at the end o' the tours. They never suspected they were being watched."

"How'd you end up pairing with them?"

"I noticed he was up to something when he kept looking at you and tugging on his ear. After you left, I wandered over acting drunk and got a bit o' info out o' Timothy while Lonnie was 'n the loo. He wasn't happy Timothy spilled the beans so he had no choice but to include me 'n their plans. You see, we knew each other from society meetings and I made them think I wasn't happy with the society anymore, just like them. When I pointed out I was your business partner and could let them know if you made any changes 'n your schedule, I was golden. They needed me for intel on you. At least that's what I convinced them to believe." Fin grinned from ear to ear.

Travis laughed as he slapped Fin on the back then tugged him into another loving hug. "You sly ole fox. You should've been a spy."

"Nay," Fin snorted, leaning back as he answered. "They work too hard. I like what we do, at our own pace and being our own bosses."

"I have to agree with you on that one," Travis said on a heavy sigh. He paused for a moment then asked, "You think they have the smarts to find us?"

"Timothy, no, but that Lonnie's a mean one. Mean don't need smarts, just dumb luck and cunning to guide their darkened hearts."

"Let's hope they guide themselves over a cliff and into the ravine long before they find their way out o' the woods." Travis brushed a kiss across Fin's brow as they reluctantly pulled apart from their hug. Before he let go completely, Travis cupped Fin through his jeans and gave a gentle squeeze. "If we weren't 'n charge o' the safety o' those two, I'd make use o' this quiet place and show you how much I've missed you."

"I know. I've missed you too. Duty first, sex later, lover." Fin teased Travis' lips with the tip of his tongue, then turned, bent over and unzipped his tent to crawl in. "Here's hoping your wish for Lonnie and Timothy comes true and they end up at the bottom o' a ravine somewhere. Wake me in a couple hours for my watch."

Travis slapped Fin's bottom playfully. The look Fin shot him was heat-filled and inviting but they both knew now wasn't the time for lust. "In that position, you strike a mighty inviting offer, but we have an obligation to fulfill first."

Before Travis turned to walk away, Fin cupped Travis, returning the loving caress, stopping him in his tracks. "When we get home, I'll hold you to that."

Travis leaned and met Fin in a passionate kiss. "You can count on it, loverboy."

* * * * *

Och! This was hard to suffer through. Thinking without the ability to act. It had nearly driven him over the edge yesterday and had caused him to wake disoriented. He couldn't let that happen again. His mind hummed, buzzing with unstoppable thoughts. Over and over, two hundred years of thoughts rushed through his head making it ache. If this didn't halt soon, he'd wish he hadn't been wakened to suffer this debilitating curse.

Man by night. Stone by day.

Insufferable damnation!

Padon tried to slow the whirlwind of ideas flashing through his skull but failed. Faces. Places. Things he'd never see again because of the length of time that had passed. MacGillivray's hate cost him everything. A life for a life. Once returned to Castle MacKinnon, he planned to find MacGillivray's descendant and end his plans to continue their dastardly evil work. Two of his *brathairs* had been freed and quite possibly a third. That's what Jasper claimed. It was the only reason Jasper allowed anyone to find him now. It was time the curse was broken. When it was, hell would not be far enough for MacGillivray's soul.

The roar rattled around his brain but never escaped his mouth. Nothing escaped.

Nothing moved. Not a finger nor a toe. He couldn't even stretch the tension from his back and shoulders. At least he'd thought to place his hands in front of his kilt to help hide his stiffened condition. It had been hard and heavy for the voluptuous Lynn before he fell to the dastardly magic of the daylight. He felt certain it remained that way as he stood locked in this stone prison.

Aye. She was lovely. Sweet. Innocent in her ways and smart as well. He liked the feel of her legs wrapped around his waist. The touch of her breasts to his back as they'd travelled through the woods kept him aware of the fact she was all woman. Perfectly proportioned for him. Her scent filled his senses bringing him a peaceful calm within his tomb and his mind stayed focused on her.

When he'd reached around to readjust her, he couldn't force his hands to release that finely shaped bottom. It pleased him she hadn't seemed to mind especially when he teased her with his thumbs. *Och*, how he wished she had been naked and his fingers could have touched her softest feminine spots. Heat from her kept his fingers warm and his thumbs active. Several instances when his movements caused her to bounce, she'd released a whispered moan. One he knew she tried to keep him from hearing, but it had made him smile and if he could, he'd be smiling right now but this damn curse refused to cooperate.

The memory of the taste of her mouth filled his and he wished he were free to plunder that tender opening once again. He'd noted how her bright blue eyes had darkened with desire yet she'd blushed and pulled away. She kissed like a practiced woman, which was something else he liked about her. He sensed she knew what she wanted in a *leannan* — lover.

A *leannan*. Aye, that would be nice to be for her. To see those eyes darken a deeper shade of blue while he explored every inch of her would be a treat, a luxury he planned to enjoy time and time again, if she let him. Padon focused on Lynn and what he'd do if he were free to make her moan his name repeatedly in pleasure.

Kissing her lips while he undressed her from her odd clothing would be an exciting feat. The men's trews would have to go. And that loose shirt would be the next to follow. The clothing of today's women was strange, yet he found them provocative on Lynn. What type of undergarments did the women of this new world wear? He'd only glimpsed them drying on a rock in the cave, but had not examined them closely. He couldn't wait to find out how they felt, while removing them from Lynn. The woman controlled his mind at the moment.

He remembered the weight of her breasts in his palms. The size of her nipples intrigued him. They were perfect for him. With the right amount of attention, he planned to caress them with his mouth, tongue, teeth and fingertips until they were pointed peaks. His mouth ached to sample those ample mounds of flesh and tease a moan from her lips.

Not stopping there, his mind wandered down her, kissing, licking and tasting every supple ounce of her flesh from her breasts down her soft and pliant tummy to the treasure between her thighs. A pirate he would be as he plundered her sweet nectar until she screamed his name and convulsed in pleasure. He could only imagine how good she would taste. Taking his time to please her until she was ready to receive him had him wishing for sundown.

Padon couldn't stop the images rolling through his thoughts even if he wanted to. Lynn's beauty surrounded him, keeping him focused on her and not the abysmal tomb of stone. The only hardness he was interested in was that between his thighs as he imagined it hovered at the entrance to her heat.

He knew if he could feel right now, he'd be stiff and tight even without being encased in stone.

Padon appeared in her dreams, gorgeously naked, and ready to please her. His kiss lit a fire in her belly. His fingertips twisted and tugged her nipples in a series of rough and soft combinations, which zinged need straight to her mound. She really liked the fact he seemed to know her breasts were a hub of nerves and when played with right could cause her to have miniature orgasms.

His lips, mouth and teeth were everywhere at once, guiding her to the edge of ecstasy and keeping her teetering, aching to plunge into the abyss of pleasure his touch promised. The lower he travelled the higher she climbed. Tickling her navel with the tip of his tongue got her even wetter and she couldn't help but spread her legs hoping he'd ease the tremendous ache.

Instead he kissed the insides of her thighs and slowly worked his way into her heat. A long gentle lick of her slit had her whining for more. She locked her hands in his hair, keeping it out of his face as he indulged. She wanted nothing to distract this talented man. Lick after lick, made her hotter.

When his tongue speared her repeatedly at a rapid pace, her orgasm hit like a tidal wave.

He lifted to kiss her and she suckled her flavor from his lips. Their kiss deepened as he slowly pushed inside her. More. She wanted more. Lifting her hips she took him in farther. She set the pace. Slow then fast. Over and over, she met his pushes and ground against him taking every inch he had to offer. Full and tight was how he made her feel and she loved it.

Padon's lips trailed to a nipple and tugged it hard between his teeth. She arched her back and screamed his name as another orgasm ripped her to the core.

"Padon!"

Lynn's eyes opened at the sound of her voice. She sat upright, breathing heavily. Wide-eyed she stared at Padon's statue and wondered if he heard her scream his name. Did Travis and Fin hear her scream? Oh Lordy, she hoped not.

She swung her legs over the side of the cot and took several deep breaths to calm herself. She'd had some rather sensual dreams in her life but nothing ever this hot and completely sexual.

On shaky legs, she stood and walked over to Padon's statue. Man, she surely hoped he hadn't heard it. How would she explain calling him when she knew he couldn't come? Come? Had he come with her in her dream? She'd woken before she knew the answer. Lynn burst out laughing. This was just plain crazy. Sex with Padon, just the thought of it had her wet and ready.

He'd called you his wee one. He said you were a treasure to be savored slowly, the little voice inside her head pointed out. Lynn shivered from head to toe. No one had ever called her a wee one, not built the way she was, plump and round in a full-figured womanly way. She shook off the idea Padon found her attractive. Self-doubt reared its ugly head and weakened her soul trying to convince her it had to be a side-effect of being cursed for so long.

Typical man, he simply woke up with morning wood.

The nasty snide voice of insecurity took over. Yes, they'd kissed. Yes, he turned her on beyond belief but once they got him home, that's where it would probably end. She had her life back in Texas. And he… He had a whole new life to learn here and she doubted it included her once he was back on familiar ground at Castle MacKinnon with his family surrounding him.

Chapter Nine

The instant the sun disappeared Lynn sensed an electric current in the air right before the stone cracked and Padon was freed. He shook remnants of the dust and pebbles from him before stepping forward, closing the distance between them. Without a word, he took her in his arms and kissed her tenderly.

"Ye were my salvation," he whispered but didn't explain because someone pounded on the door.

"Are you ready to go?" Travis called. "We've got a good bit o' ground to cover to reach Fin's grandpa's house."

"'Til later, my wee one." He brushed a quick kiss to her forehead then stepped past her to open the door. "Aye. We be ready."

His words tickled her to the core, but confused her still the same. His actions renewed her lust for him but how was *she* his salvation? When he turned in the doorway and held his hand to her, she couldn't miss the intensity in his gaze. It gave her goose bumps just looking at him. Strands of his hair hung in his eyes giving him a bad boy appeal. She took his hand and they followed Travis and Fin.

Her nerves were on edge from lack of sleep. After that magnificent dream, she'd spent the rest of the day pacing the cabin, going outside only to relieve herself or to get a bit of fresh air. Every noise she heard added to the edginess. On occasion, Travis or Fin dropped by to bring her food and check on her and make sure she and Padon were safe. She wondered if they, too, found it odd that nothing was seen or heard of from Lonnie and Timothy.

Were those two lost in the woods? Had they taken off when Jasper put a scare into Timothy? Something in her gut whispered *that* didn't happen. Those two were unpredictable as far as she was concerned. And unpredictable made them dangerous.

She didn't like that once they cleared the woods it was open terrain for the rest of the trek to the farmhouse. The full moon gave them great visibility but also made them an easy target. It was obvious the men didn't like it either. Fin stayed on point and Travis brought up the rear. Padon kept her close and never stopped scouting the area for any sign of possible attack. With the three of them around her, she doubted anyone would make the mistake of messing with them. But anything was possible.

A sigh of relief escaped when she first saw the MacIntyre's farmhouse. A light was on in the rear of the house and Fin pointed out it was the kitchen. His grandfather spent many nights sitting at the table, drinking tea and reading the local news before bed. He commonly left the light on for Fin, when he knew Fin was in the area. With Fin's car in the driveway, he probably figured Fin and Travis were hunting or fishing. Fin liked to spend as much time as possible with his grandfather, especially since his grandmother passed away several years ago. When he wasn't working or staying with Travis in Edinburgh, he was here.

Fin opened the unlocked door and stepped inside. The others followed. The kitchen was empty. He came to a halt pointing to the paper on the floor by the chair and the cup of tea sitting untouched on the table. When he tugged the knife from the sheath at his hip, Padon followed suit drawing his sword.

"It is not like grandpa to leave a mess or a full cup," Fin whispered with a nod toward the table then switched off the light to make them less visible to whoever was in the house.

Padon nodded then turned to Lynn placing a finger to his lips then motioning for her to stay put. Fear sliced through her. What was going on? Was someone in the house who wasn't supposed to be there? She stepped backwards until she leaned into the corner of the cabinets and the wall containing the back door. The shadows swallowed her; at least, that's what she hoped. Padon winked then took his place beside Fin and Travis at the door leading into the front room.

"When we go through the door," Fin whispered. He nodded at Travis. "You take the dining room to the left." He looked at Padon. "You take the room to the right and I'll clear the hallway and entrance."

The three of them glided through the door one at a time each slinking off in their appointed direction. A swinging door inside the kitchen to the left slowly opened and a man snuck in. It had to be the dining room where Travis had just entered through the hallway door. Whoever was hiding there moved through the second door and into the kitchen. As he maneuvered toward the door that led to the hallway from the kitchen, it appeared to Lynn as if he planned to attack them from behind. She couldn't let that happen.

Frantically she looked around for a weapon. Grabbing the only thing she saw, a cutting board, she quietly walked up behind him and before he made a move, she whacked him on the head. He crumbled to his knees and landed face first in the doorway holding his head and whimpering.

Travis reached in through the swinging door and flipped the light switch. Padon stood over the moaning man, who rolled onto his back. Timothy lay sprawled out at their feet.

"My head, oh my head," Timothy whined.

Fin returned from searching the rest of the house. When he saw Timothy on the floor, he dropped to one knee, fisted the front of his shirt and jerked him upward. Sneering in his face, he demanded, "Where's my grandfather?"

"Lonnie has him," Timothy gasped without letting go of his head.

"Where?" Fin growled between clenched teeth.

"Not telling you." Timothy groaned. "You got to give Lonnie what you found 'n the cave if you want your grandfather back."

Padon reached around Fin and dragged Timothy to his feet. He slammed Timothy's back against the doorjamb. The man dangled like a damp rag in the wind. No matter how hard he stretched, his feet wouldn't touch the ground as Padon held him firmly in place with one hand, while pressing the tip of the sword to his throat.

"I believe *m'caraid* asked ye a question. Answer and be spared disembowelment."

"Dis—," Timothy stuttered. "Disembowelment?"

From the look on his face, Lynn doubted he knew what the word meant but feared Padon's threat anyway. She studied Padon for a long few seconds. Would he or wouldn't he slit the man open and gut him like a fish? Not a good thing to have to explain to the authorities. Not realizing she still held the cutting board in her hand, she stepped closer. Timothy flinched at the sight of her and she swallowed the smile. He feared her as well. Maybe she could use this to their advantage.

"Timothy," she said in an even-keeled tone. Lynn put on her best stern face and stared directly at the shivering man. "Do you understand how much trouble you already are in for kidnapping me?" He shook his head and she believed he didn't realize what might happen to him. "If I report you and Lonnie to the police, you will go to jail. Now that the two of you have committed another kidnapping that will be considered your second offense and you'll be sentenced to an even longer term." She looked at Travis. "About how long do you think the Scottish courts will give them for something like this?"

"At least twenty years," Travis answered in a deadpan tone without cracking a smile. "Maybe more considering they took an American hostage and they damn near got her killed."

"Hostage. Killed," Timothy blurted. "We didn't kill anyone. She's standing right there."

Lynn adjusted the cutting board and Timothy leaned back tight against the doorjamb and looked as if he wished he could run. "You're right. I'm not dead but you and your friend put my life in danger. I fell off a cliff and rolled ass over teakettle into a deep ravine. I could've died and I think that'll make a valid impression on the court." She shot a quick look at Padon who stood with a steady hand on the sword at Timothy's throat and a look of pure menace in his eyes. If she were on the wrong end of that sword, she'd be scared to breathe.

She gave Timothy as hard a glare as she could muster and hoped this worked. "If you want leniency for any of your actions, it would be in your best interest to tell us where your partner is hiding."

"He'll kill me," Timothy gasped.

"Death now," Padon stated, gliding the tip of his sword gently up Timothy's neck to stop at his chin, "or later. Ye choose. At my hand, death shall be agonizingly painful. At the hand o' a friend, ye may stand a chance o' survival or a quick, less messy end ifn' he be a true *cariad*. Choose wisely."

Fin hovered beside Timothy and added just the right ingredients to the mix to tip the scale in their favor. "Think it through, Tim. Who got their hands dirty the most taking her captive? We did. Who carried her up the mountain? We did. Who did he drop over the side o' a cliff into the unknown o' a cave? You. Who did he leave behind to get beat up or killed when we arrived?"

Lynn saw a bead of sweat trickle down the side of Timothy's face. It appeared as if he digested every word before saying, "Me. Lonnie left me behind."

"A true friend leaves no one behind to face a posse of danger. He could've left a note for us, detailing what he wanted," Travis piped in.

Every ounce of color drained from Timothy's face. On a hoarse whisper he repeated, "He could've left a note. Instead he left me."

Lynn cupped Timothy's cheek. "Tell us where to find Fin's grandfather and I won't tell the authorities you were a part of this."

Timothy swallowed hard and his head bobbed like a dashboard doll's. "Aye. I'll tell you what you want to know."

After much discussion, the strategy had been agreed upon and their path set in motion. Timothy explained that Fin's grandfather and Lonnie were picked up by several members of this new group they'd joined run by someone named Brother Leod and taken to Edinburgh. Padon insisted they rescue Fin's grandfather before returning him home. Fin's grandfather was in danger. Padon's homecoming could wait until the elder was safe.

The three of them had been careful not to explain to Timothy what had been found in the cave. They made him think it was an object of great value and not a MacKinnon statue. Padon thought it odd this Brother Leod, this supposed leader of their group, would not choose wiser men for his brigade. Timothy never clued in, even with how Padon was dressed that he was the object in question. Travis claimed him to be his cousin and Timothy simply accepted it. Padon shook his head. Either Timothy was truly not bright or plain scared witless by his current situation.

A glance to the stars and he knew which direction was home. Turning north, he stared long and hard as if he could conjure the image of the castle in front of his eyes if he concentrated. Two hundred years had passed. What were a few more days? He sighed.

It startled him to see Travis and Fin shove Timothy into the belly of some sort of odd-shaped beast. Then they, too, climbed into the front compartment of it. It roared to life and its eyes opened, shooting out bright beams of light. In a split second, his hand found his sword and prepared to attack, but seeing the men inside unharmed as they waved made him hesitate and drop his hand to his side.

"That's Fin's car," Lynn stated as if that was supposed to soothe him. It didn't.

He'd listened earlier when Fin explained he'd driven to the farm with Lonnie and Timothy then tracked them into the woods. The how they'd gotten there hadn't sunken in until now.

He swallowed his confusion and the multitude of questions barreling through his brain. So many new things surrounded him. The inside of the house with its magical overhead lights, its running water in something called a sink and a stove that heated without wood for a fire. So much to learn his head hurt from the effort.

He followed Lynn as she walked away from the object that confined the men. When she stopped at a smaller, yet similar, beast and opened its side, his gut knotted. Was she getting in this thing? Did she expect him to as well? From the look of it, she did. Padon dug deep hoping not to show his disdain for this new object.

Her touch to his arm soothed some of his angst as she smiled at him. If this petite beauty had no fear of this metal beast then he would trust her instincts and do as she did in order to overcome this minor obstacle in his pathway home.

The gentle rub she gave his wrist made him smile as her soft twang floated to his ears. Concern filled her words. "Are you okay? There's so much that has changed since you've been cursed. I'm willing to help you learn about some of the things you need to live in this world. Beginning with this." She pointed to the car as she continued, "It's a car. I rented it when I arrived at the airport. We use it to travel instead of a flesh and blood horse. Consider it a mechanical horse that takes you places at greater speeds than a real horse."

He lifted her hand to his lips and kissed it. "Lynn, if ye say this me—chan—ical," he stumbled over the word as he spoke, "horse be safe then it be as ye say. I trust ye, my wee one."

Her face flushed with color as she wiggled her hand from his. The spark of fire in her gaze even though she blushed from his words made him even more curious to learn her every nuance. When she moved, he couldn't help but watch her.

"You need to take off your sword to fit in the seat." She opened the rear door of this beast and held her hands out for him to pass it to her.

There was no hesitation as he slipped it over his head but he didn't give it to her. A grin brightened his face. "My wee one, my sword be very heavy."

She cocked her head to the side and he liked the cute arched eyebrow look she shot him. It appeared his wee one had a playful nature. "How heavy could it be?"

He laid it in her open hands without releasing it completely. Both of her hands automatically lowered as she tried to hold it steady. A surprised laugh escaped as she agreed. "No wonder your arms are so big. This thing is solid."

He brushed a kiss across her brow then leaned in and placed it where she indicated. She shut the door and showed him to the front seat. Lynn bent over and pushed the seat as far away from the dashboard as possible. Padon couldn't pull his eyes away from the delectable roundness of her bottom. His palms ached to fondle its softness. When she straightened and turned it was all he could do not to show the guilt of his thoughts upon his face.

Och, the woman made him randy as a young buck in mating season.

"Hopefully this will give you enough room," she said as her gaze swept from his feet to his head. "But I doubt it."

When he got settled on the seat, she reached across him and showed him how to operate the seatbelt. She closed the door behind him and scooted to the driver's side.

Her scent permeated his senses when she'd reached across to strap him. If the others were not waiting for them, he would've taken her in his arms and ravished her mouth like a hungry animal.

Padon watched her move in front of the metal beast. He liked the sexy little jiggle of her breasts as she walked with purpose. Closing his eyes, he leaned into the seat. The image of her standing in the kitchen doorway over Timothy as she held a board in her hand made his lips twitch into a smile. She'd knocked him on his arse with one blow. Now that was a woman.

She'd tried to carry his Claymore but it was too heavy for a wee one like her. The fact she'd even attempted showed she didn't fear weapons. Perhaps after he returned to Castle MacKinnon, he'd locate a fine sword smith and commission a special dagger for this spitfire o' a lass. It would be a perfect gift in his opinion.

His eyes sprang open the moment the beast beneath him roared to life. Lynn pulled a lever and the mechanical horse moved. Padon's heart thumped inside his chest as he gripped the seat. His knees pressed against the inside of the beast's stomach and he wished he had more room to maneuver. In this position, he couldn't reach his sword quickly enough if trouble arose.

Her hand grasped his causing him to look her way. She gave him a quick smile right before she stared straight to the beast in front of them. "We will be fine, Padon. Relax. I'm a good driver. I promise."

Relax. How 'n the name o' the angels was he going to relax while riding 'n the belly o' a metal beast? He turned his eyes forward and was stunned to see the beast in front of them also had red glowing eyes on its arse. Was it angry they followed so closely?

Lynn drove but couldn't keep her thoughts off the hunk next to her. In the house, she'd noted Padon had studied his surroundings carefully as if taking mental notes of every detail. He'd remained quiet and didn't ask questions though she knew he must have had a zillion running through his brain. Standing next to the car, she caught the first visible signs of distress in him since the cave when Jasper had to leave. She saw the fear in his eyes as she opened the passenger side door for him.

It tore at her heart to see him this disconcerted. Big and bad mixed with vulnerable and scared made him even more hunky in her eyes. She did her best to help soothe his nerves by rubbing his wrist. The touch may have helped calm him, but it did nothing to ease the jumble of sensations zinging through her belly. The way he stared intently at her and the deep resonance in his sexy baritone as he called her his *wee one* sent a thrill down her spine to pool in-between her thighs. The more he called her that, the more it set her insides all aflutter and turned her mind to mush.

She did her best to make him comfortable in the car and hoped she didn't have to hit the brakes hard, because it would probably crush his knees in the dashboard. Out of the corner of her eye, she saw his fear reignite when she started the car. Maybe he was feeling claustrophobic being cramped in such a small space. Lynn pressed the control for the window and he jumped the instant it opened.

"I'm sorry, Padon," Lynn said as she explained. "I thought you'd like some air so I lowered the window for you." She shot him a quick smile, as she looked his way for a moment, before returning her gaze to the road. "I should've warned you."

He leaned his head out like a joyful dog on a car ride. The grip he had on the seat eased and his hands moved to his lap. After several minutes, he pulled his head in and leaned back in a more restful position. He turned to her and smiled. "Thank ye, milady. Fresh air helped."

"You're welcome."

Even though the night air was cool, her skin was flushed. Damn. She couldn't believe how he managed to get her hot without more than a couple of well-spoken words and a few stolen quick kisses to her brow and her lips. Just remembering how those felt made her nipples tingle. She prayed for the ability to resist jumping his bones. Oh Lordy, she rolled her eyes heavenward. Something about this man brought out the naughtiest of thoughts and had her wishing she were a bad, bad girl.

"This car be fast."

His comment jarred her from her thoughts. "Umm, yes. It's faster than the average horse." She cleared her throat and did her best to start a conversation she thought would help him understand more about today's world. "It has what's called an engine which makes it go. The engine requires fuel to work." An idea popped into her head and she ran with it. "Kind of like a horse. You had to feed and water a horse to keep them healthy and make them work. Right?"

"Aye." He nodded.

"With a car, the engine is its stomach and it eats fuel in order to work."

"And ye drive it instead o' guide it with reins like a horse," Padon added and she sensed he seemed more at ease as they spoke.

"Yes," she answered. "The steering wheel is how I guide it and I use the foot pedals to make it go and stop."

Again he nodded and she noted his unease lessened even more. If she kept the conversation going, hopefully he'd be more comfortable with the car by the time they reached their destination. With only a few hours of night left, the first stop in this rescue mission was Travis' place in Edinburgh. They needed a location to hide Padon during the day and be closer to where Timothy claimed Lonnie had taken Fin's grandfather.

Out of the corner of her eye, she checked the side mirror then shot her gaze to the rearview. Nothing shone in the night. No additional headlights followed them. Still she couldn't shake the sensation someone or something was back there. She breathed deep trying to calm the unease. It had to be the situation that kept her nerves taut and on edge. She did her best to focus on Padon and their conversation which helped make the time pass quickly.

She enjoyed listening to his sexy brogue as he spoke of his family. The dedication and love couldn't be missed in his voice. Keeping him talking about his home seemed to ease most of the tension from him, but she sensed a deep sadness laced every word. It had to be difficult to wake up and learn life passed you by while you slept, cursed in a stone tomb. Lynn tried not to dwell on that aspect as she did her best to keep him focused on a subject he knew and understood — his family. Before she knew it they were pulling into the driveway of Travis' home in Edinburgh.

The sun threatened to breach the sky as she hurried Padon into the cottage behind Travis. He motioned to the first open door off the hallway. It was the bedroom where she'd left her things before they'd started their camping trip to find a ghost with a secret. She eyed Padon. What a hell of a secret Jasper protected for centuries.

Chapter Ten

It hurt her heart to watch him fall to the curse again. He stood proud and staring at her with a heat that warmed her to her toes. A longing to hold him, kiss and make love to him grew in every fiber of her being. She wanted desperately to learn how to break this curse for good. Lynn pressed her palm flat to his chest and swore she felt his heartbeat. Even if it wasn't possible, it didn't matter. As long as she believed it, then to her it was true. His heart still beat beneath that heavy stone tomb and that gave her hope he was alive.

Travis and Fin locked Timothy in a closet just to be safe. Neither of them trusted Timothy even though they doubted he had the capability of planning an escape without his cohort Lonnie. Even with him locked away, Lynn still had a dreadful feeling in the pit of her stomach something wasn't right. The look Timothy shot her right before they'd closed the closet door gave her chills.

Lynn tried to relax. She took a shower and lingered in the water until she was pruned. Still it didn't help ease the nagging discomfort that something balanced in the wings waiting to happen the moment she lowered her guard. Wrapped in a towel, she crossed the room passing Padon in the process.

Could he see her? She stood in front of him, dropped the towel and did a sexy stroll around him. Her fingertips lightly caressed him as she moved, giving her a sensation of closeness even though a thick layer of stone separated them. Unable to resist, she jiggled her breasts wishing Padon would touch them, hold them and taste them until she couldn't take it anymore. When he didn't, disappointment settled in her gut even though she didn't really expect him to move until sundown.

She turned, drew the shade shutting out the sunlight and then closed the curtains for an added measure of darkness. Lynn slipped on her pajamas. The moment she snuggled under the covers, she realized it appeared as if Padon stood watch over her. His hands were crossed at his waist. His back straight, chin lifted and his gaze — though frozen — still focused on her never letting her out of his sight. Silly as it may seem, a sense of security flowed within her, lulling her to sleep.

Complete exhaustion didn't keep her from dreaming of Padon. If she had her way, he'd be beside her, wrapped around her instead of standing guard across the room.

His heat would keep her warm. His lips would turn her on and… Oh Lordy, he'd do things to her she'd long forgotten about since the death of her husband.

Deeper into sleep, she hungered for his touch to the point her dream made her believe he was right beside her. Touching her. Caressing her. Kissing her. Tongue upon tongue, lip upon lip. His flavor inspired her hunger to crave more and more of his kiss. She instantly responded. Both nipples hardened. Her abdominal muscles flinched as the phantom sensation of his fingers feather-light touches teased her. Moisture formed between her thighs as her hidden bud tightened with a desperate ache.

In slow motion, his fingers worked their magic, drawing tiny circles on her lower abdomen along that sensitive skin without dropping lower where she wanted them. Lower. She wanted him to touch her between her folds and finger her to completion. But he didn't.

His lips never left hers. His hands caressed and touched, teasing and strumming her to perfection until every uncovered section of skin sizzled from his ministrations. Lynn's moan broke their kiss. Unable to take anymore, she grabbed his wrist and guided his hand where she desperately needed his attention. He cupped her mound and she sighed, breathing deeply as her legs opened wide.

His fingers needed no further guidance. Back and forth, he slid them along her slit causing her to become more and more wet. In. She wanted him in her. She'd take whatever he'd give her for some form of relief. Time after time, he came close to but didn't enter her. Lynn lifted her pelvis from the bed urging him to fulfill her need. Unwilling to take anymore teasing, she intertwined her fingers with his and showed them what she wanted.

In deep. Out until just the tips hovered within her entrance, then in deep again. Over and over, she helped him set the pace as she held his wrist while his fingers did the walking. She needed. Oh Lordy, did she need. Faster and faster, she pumped her hips in tune to his fingers. One solid swirl of his thumb to her clit and she bit back the scream of ecstasy as her back arched and a wave of pure pleasure took her over the edge. Her clit throbbed as her cream soaked his fingers.

At last, she groaned. Release at last.

He stood watching her masturbate. Was she dreaming? Apparently she was, but he really didn't care. What he came for wasn't her. It stood in the corner, poised and quite ripe for the taking. His boss would be proud.

Ignoring her passion-riddled moans in the background, he perused his prize. Frozen. Lifeless. This was easier than taking candy from a child. The MacKinnon looked extremely heavy in this latent form. That mattered not to him. He had plenty of support to carry out his plan. It had been easy enough to convince his partner to go along with it. The idiot listened to every word and absorbed them like they were his own to act upon. The plan had gone without a hitch and here he stood ready to redeem his reward.

A smile tugged at his lips but he refused to allow it. Not yet anyway, not until the job was done. Slow and deliberate he walked toward the bed. She lay entangled in the blankets. Her face was flushed from her dream.

It must've been a really hot one. If he had the time to spare, he'd help her with her little problem. Time was something he didn't have. They were supposed to have delivered the MacKinnon by now. Brother Leod was becoming impatient. But what was he to do? His partner was incompetent and unreliable so he'd made other arrangements, which no longer included him.

What a shame, they'd been friends for years.

With a damp cloth in hand, he silently closed the distance to the bed. She never knew what hit her. Just like what happened with Travis and Fin. Neither had a chance to respond before the drug claimed them. Her eyes opened wide, but he doubted she had time to focus before the chloroform took effect and slammed them shut. With the last one out of the way, he pulled the cell phone from his pocket and made the call.

"Transport needed. Problem secured."

* * * * *

"Lynn, wake up, lass."

Someone shook her hard while calling her name. Her head felt like a sack of bricks sat on it. When she swallowed, her mouth was the driest it had ever been and a horrid taste coated her tongue. What the hell happened?

A face appeared behind her eyes and instantly she bolted upright. Unbelievable.

Grasping for any form of saliva she could muster, she sputtered, "Timothy. He—"

"We know, lass," Travis replied coldly. "He got the drop on all of us. Fin and I just woke from whatever he used on us."

Lynn stared at the empty corner. "Padon?"

"He took him," Fin stated from the doorway. "Don't you fear, lass. We will be getting him back."

"How'd he get out of the closet?" Lynn questioned in a panic as she tested her legs before she stood. Her head spun but she managed to gain her balance.

"Seems we were duped." Travis cupped her elbow for support. "From what we've figured out, Lonnie was hiding in the trunk of Fin's car. We found the backseat pushed out. They must've loosened it in order for Lonnie to escape from the trunk, then he freed Timothy from the closet. Apparently, our capturing Timothy was part of their grand plan."

"Gentlemen." She looked to the doorway to see an older version of Fin standing behind his left shoulder. She could only assume he was Fin's grandfather. With a nod in her direction, he added, "and lassie. We have a problem. Seems Timothy cut his ties to Lonnie."

They followed Thicket MacIntyre into the kitchen. "Lass, you may want to be looking away."

When she shook her head, he opened the pantry door. Lonnie's lifeless body lay crammed in the small space. His neck was obviously broken. Lynn gasped and said a prayer for his soul. Timothy's face was the last she'd seen before she'd been drugged. The nagging little voice in the back of her head whispered, *I told you so. I told you something wasn't right.*

It surprised her that her brain functioned enough to form a sentence. "Where were you?" She poised her question to Fin's grandfather.

"The bastards knocked on the door. Since I knew them from the society to protect the MacKinnons, I made the mistake o' opening the door. They overpowered me and used the same drug on me as they used on you. When I woke up, I discovered I was in a car trunk. I just kept pounding on the lid until Fin and Travis here found me."

She looked from Fin to Travis. "He was in your trunk the whole time," Travis answered. Her jaw dropped. She knew she'd felt like something or someone was behind her last night as she drove, she just didn't know how close he truly had been. They'd never even considered opening the trunks. They'd had no reason to. Timothy played them for fools. He'd given a prize-winning performance in her opinion. The idiot at their mercy wasn't an idiot at all but the mastermind behind the pair. Damn! She felt like such a fool and now Padon was in jeopardy.

In his current condition, he had no defenses. Lynn's gut flipped and knotted. They had to find him before Timothy turned him over to this madman or worse, smashed him while stuck in statue form.

* * * * *

"Well done, Timothy," Brother Leod commended as he circled the MacKinnon. "You have succeeded where others have failed before you."

"Thank you, master," Timothy replied. He held his stance taut and his face showed none of the excitement that roared through his veins. It was all he could do not to smile at his own achievement.

"You have proven your worth to me and you shall be rewarded." He watched Brother

Leod continue to peruse the statue as if looking for a particular mark to prove its validity as being the right one.

Brother Leod turned to face him. Timothy shuddered inwardly at the sight of the marred left side of his face. It was crinkled as if he'd been caught in a fire. There was no eyebrow above his left eye and that gave him an eerie appearance. Those golden, wheat-colored eyes seemed to swirl as their stares met. The sensation of falling filtered through him and he actually grabbed the wall beside him for support. But he wasn't moving. Timothy couldn't pull his gaze from Brother Leod's powerful control. A presence entered his head, tapping into his thoughts, shuffling through them like a deck of cards.

When he was done, Brother Leod turned away from Timothy, releasing him from his mental snare. Timothy physically shook trying to regain his composure. Anger built him a backbone and he lunged toward Leod and grabbed his shoulder, forcing him to turn back around.

"What the hell was that about?"

Leod's right eyebrow arched. "I had to know if you were trustworthy or if this was a trick."

"I got rid o' Lonnie to prove my devotion to the cause," he snapped. "That should have been enough. *That* and the fact I brought you the damn MacKinnon you asked for."

A wicked smile upturned Leod's lips. Timothy forced his eyes not to meet Leod's magical gaze again. He looked at his nose, lips or his chin but not his eyes. It bothered him this man had some sort of magical power of mind control.

"And for that you shall be paid." Brother Leod nodded toward the big redheaded goon of a guy, who stood stoic beside the only piece of furniture in the room, an old wooden desk. "Roy, give our loyal follower of the Brotherhood of the Sons of the Servant of Judgment his due payment."

Roy opened a briefcase on the desk and pulled out a manila envelope. He walked over to Timothy and handed it to him. Timothy quickly peeked inside and saw two neatly bundled stacks of money. Both were for him. With Lonnie gone, he didn't have to share.

"There's more where that came from," Brother Leod stated, "*if* you find me another MacKinnon statue. From my calculations, there are three cursed brothers left. You have proven yourself to be an asset to our cause. Don't let me down."

Timothy no longer tried to hide his smile as he folded the envelope and shoved it in the inside pocket of his jacket. "Consider the statues as good as found."

"Roy here will walk you out." Brother Leod waved a hand at Roy then turned back to studying the statue.

"Don't you worry. I'll find you another one o' those statues," Timothy boasted as Roy escorted him through the door.

When he returned, Roy stood beside Brother Leod. "I don't see why you like that one."

"I don't," Brother Leod replied coldly. "But *he* got the job done." He shot a sideways look at Roy. "Now don't you worry, Roy. You'll get your chance to do with him whatever you wish once the last cursed MacKinnon is in my possession."

Roy snickered as he punched his fist in his palm and Brother Leod knew from past experiences Roy liked to inflict severe pain before he killed.

"Do I get a chance at him too?" Doc stood in the doorway adjusting his wire-rimmed glasses and grinning as if waiting for his cue to go after the young man. Strands of white hair hung in his face and his frame was so thin it looked as if he hadn't eaten in a decade. His beady black eyes seemed to sparkle in delight at the thoughts of the things he'd like to do to Timothy if given the chance. Fucking him raw would be the first on Doc's agenda. Leod didn't doubt that for a minute.

"I'm sure you and Roy can work something out." He nodded at Doc. "As long as you made it painful."

"Painful pleasure, oh yes," he practically drooled as his voice squeaked.

Brother Leod shook his head, watching Doc turn and leave. Between the pain Roy would inflict by beating Timothy and the sexual pain Doc would treat his patient to, Timothy would either die happy from the ass fucking or die a broken and beaten man. He cared neither which way as long as Timothy didn't fail to bring him another MacKinnon. If he did, his days would be drastically numbered when he unleashed those two on him.

"Leave me," Brother Leod commanded and Roy did as ordered.

Dragging his hand along the stone as he circled it again, excitement brewed. It had been a long time coming. Three failures so far. He'd come so close twice. Those attempts had cost him his pretty boy looks. Absently, he touched the taut, twisted left side of his face then dropped his hand to his hip. The third time, he'd never even gotten near the statue before it had been set free. He'd felt the sizzle in the air and knew another MacKinnon had been awakened, but it wasn't until he saw the idiot antiquities thief arrested on the news that he knew of another one's location.

By then, it was too late.

The MacKinnon had met his mate and the curse was broken. Not this time. Leod snickered looking at the dead eyes of the statue. This time he'd succeeded and captured a statue. According to Timothy, someone had spoken the anti-curse and set him free. Leod couldn't help but grin. That was half a freedom.

What will he think when he awakes and sees me? Nightfall couldn't come fast enough.

"Ah," he sighed. Things were finally falling into place. The prophecy would be fulfilled and the Book of Shadows would be his to command.

Power rippled through his veins and his fingers warmed and glowed. Flames danced on his fingertips then disappeared as quickly as they'd been summoned. Mind control and keeper of the eternal flame were his specialties. So far, those tricks had not been enough to gain him the book.

He had to fulfill the prophecy set in motion over two hundred years ago by his great ancestor and namesake, Hume Leod MacGillivray. Leod's new strategy seemed to be his best. Find and steal the remaining cursed MacKinnons and use them as bait to capture the other MacKinnon brothers. Having them all locked in one location would make it so much easier to kill them.

Though his plan to destroy the statues had taken a different path, he still planned to rid the world of this particular MacKinnon clan. The one brother at a time strategy had not been successful. Now he hungered to annihilate them all in one dastardly blow or at least most of them for now and the other three once they were found. He grinned. With that completed, the monks who hid and protected the Book of Shadows would have no choice but to fulfill his ancestor's dying wishes.

Whoever shall vanquish Clan MacKinnon shall be thy keeper o' thy Book o' Shadows for all eternity.

A big book chock full of black magic spells and an eternity to practice them all on an unsuspecting world. Now that was a dream come true. Brother Leod's maniacal laughter bounced off the walls. He had no worry of anyone hearing him. Where they were located was a long forgotten station on a pier once used for ferries across the water. The ferries stopped years ago and the pier's dire need of repairs condemned it for use. Use by anyone else, that is. Leod grinned as he lifted the edge of the dirty curtain that hung over the smudged and broken window.

Not a person within line-of-sight or earshot. This place was perfect for what he had in mind. A Viking send-off of sorts for a Scottish clan of brothers.

Chapter Eleven

Images of her kept him sane while condemned to stone. Her beauty filled the space behind his eyes and calmed him when otherwise his mind would have revolted against its prison as the walls closed in on him. Lynn's smile brought him inner joy and the wonders of her body set his imagination ablaze with sexual scenarios he wanted to experience with her. Thinking of the bed he'd seen in the room before his eyes closed fueled his desire to explore Lynn's supple shape in every position possible.

Och! His body may not have the ability to react but his mind hummed with vibrant visions of him and her naked, wrapped together as one. He knew if he were not cursed, his shaft would be more solid than the stone that held him tight at that moment. He hungered to taste her lips the second he was set free. If he were a lucky man, he'd sample the flavor of the haven between her thighs if she allowed him. In the throes of passion, he bet she tasted sweeter than the bee's honey.

Pleasure. He wanted nothing more than to bring her to her pleasure time and time again before he entered her, bringing them both to the precipice of desire only to tumble into the abyss of glorious release. *Och*! His bawls hung heavy between his thighs desperate to spill his seed deep within Lynn's treasure.

She wasn't an innocent yet she seemed innocent to him in many ways. Her beautiful blush turned him on with each touch or kiss he'd given her. The heat in her eyes spoke of experience and added to his growing excitement about this provocative woman. He wanted to read her like his favorite book, learning something new each flip of the page and keep her high upon a shelf to savor repeatedly and protect from harm. His heart grew thinking about her.

Padon woke to unfamiliar surroundings. Instantly, he knew Lynn was no longer near. From the smell in the air, he knew he was close to water but how did he get there? Where was Lynn? He drew his sword and moved cautiously. The floor beneath him creaked and he stopped. Silence was important if he wanted to survey his location without being seen.

He took a breath and placed his next step carefully. With precise actions, he made his way to the window, lifted the dirty curtain and peeked out. Night had fallen which he knew since he was free. Bars covered the windows and the glass from the panes was missing or broken. Was he in a prison of sorts? Lights darted the coastline of a river. Which river, he couldn't be certain considering he didn't know where he'd been taken.

The door behind him creaked and he spun around, readying for attack. Sword held poised to protect himself. The sight of the man who entered took him by surprise. The man was dressed from head to toe in the guise of a monk. Was he or wasn't he a man of the cloth? The last time a man in such attire stood before him, Padon and his *brathairs* had been cursed. Now he chose to side with caution and kept his wits about him and his suspicions geared on high.

"Who are ye?" Padon demanded, not taking his eyes of the odd-looking man.

"I am Brother Leod." He brushed the hood from his head and Padon stiffened.

The left side of his face was marred. His ear lay folded over. His cheek a crinkled mess and his left eyebrow no longer existed. This man suffered a bad burn, which scarred half of his face while leaving the right side untouched. From the untouched side, he appeared to have been a handsome man at some point in his past. His eyes contained an eerie golden-wheat color and gut instinct told him not to stare into them for any length of time. They did not look real. There would be no trusting this individual.

Padon cleared his throat. He recognized the name as an associate of Timothy and Lonnie's, but decided it best to keep that knowledge to himself. "Where hath ye brought me? And why? Where be Lynn?"

A sinister smile upturned the supposed monk's lips and Padon sensed trouble lived within this one. He was no man of the cloth.

"You need not worry about this Lynn person. I'd be more concerned about your family and yourself." He waved a hand in the air and heat filled the room. With each fluid motion, the temperature increased.

Sweat beaded Padon's brow, but he refused to back down or believe this man held the ability to control the weather. It had to be a trick of some sort. In the car, Lynn had shown him a system that made it warm or cold depending on the passenger's needs. Was he somehow operating a similar object he had hidden within his robe? Padon stood steady and watched for the opportune moment to turn the events in his favor.

The door opened more and a rather large man with red hair walked in to stand behind Brother Leod. Padon chose to move, placing both men in direct path of his sword should the need to use it arise. Neither appeared to be carrying a weapon. And if Brother Leod thought for a second his childish tricks would alarm him, then Leod was mistaken. It took more than a bit o' heat to unnerve him.

The large redhead pulled his shoulders back and flexed his thick biceps. Padon's lip curled at the corner. Preening for a fight only showed one's weaknesses. Padon held fast his position, ignoring the sweaty sensation coating every ounce of flesh including his palms. When the oversized oaf took a step toward Padon, he twirled the sword showing he had the skill of a true swordsman. The guy's eyes widened but he wasn't bright enough to adhere to the warning. He lunged at Padon, trying to take him out at the waist by wrapping his arms around Padon. Seeing the man had no visible weapon, Padon chose not to run him through with the sword.

The impact caused him to take a step back to steady himself. Out of the corner of his eye, he noted Brother Leod sidestepped toward the desk, flipped it on its side and stood behind it as if he would use it as a shield to crouch behind if need be. Coward. Not a valiant quality in a supposed leader of men.

Padon swung around, throwing the redhead off-balance then brought his fist along with the hilt of his sword against his attacker's head. It was an efficient enough blow to cause the man's arms to instantly release him as he fell with a heavy thud to the floor. He wasn't out, simply stunned and dazed. He staggered to his feet and started swinging aimlessly. Not one blow connected with Padon, who had sheathed his sword and took to hand-to-hand since the man was neither armed with a weapon nor wits.

A right, then a left whooshed past Padon's face as he bobbed from side to side. "My *piuthar* fights better than ye," Padon taunted and watched confused anger tighten his opponent's features. It seemed too easy with this one, to the point he should feel guilty, but he didn't. It'd been way too long since he'd had a good brawl and though this guy lacked adequate fighting skills, it was better than nothing.

The man growled and threw his heavy body weight behind his next series of punches. Padon caught his fists in his hands, grinned at the man's shocked expression then head butted him. The redhead's eyes crossed and he dropped to his knees. Padon let go of his hands and the man didn't move.

He sat there dazed and confused, rocking from side to side in super slow motion.

He took a step away from his opponent, knowing the fight was over. Out of the corner of his eye, a flash of light had him spinning to face Brother Leod. His jaw dropped as he saw the man's fingertips glowing right before a ball of flames shot at him. He tried to dodge it but wasn't quick enough. It hit him in the shoulder with such force he was knocked off his feet and landed hard on his back. Burning pain made his arm twitch uncontrollably. He grabbed his elbow to try and stop it. The back of his head hurt from where it had collided with the floor but he had no time for aches and pains no matter how severe. He had a demon to kill.

Dragging himself to his feet, he released his arm and drew his sword with his uninjured hand. Intense heat filtered through the steel and the blade glowed red-hot, but he held tight though his palm begged him to release it. The evil man stood between him and the injured redhead who crawled from the room. Leod stepped backwards each time Padon took a step in his direction. It was obvious he was working his way to the door as soon as his companion had cleared it. Once they both were in the hallway, the door slammed shut between Padon and his enemies.

"Run ye cowards," Padon shouted through the wooden door as he heard the locks clicked in place.

"I am no coward," Brother Leod stated clearly and loudly. "I choose to keep you alive as bait for your brothers. Soon I shall succeed in ridding the world of your despicable clan where my ancestor miserably failed."

Padon pressed his ear against the door and heard the echo of his footsteps fade away. The heat in his sword instantly disappeared. He straightened. Looking at his hand, there were no permanent burns, simply an ache from holding fast to the hilt. A trick. The bastard had played some form of mind trick on him making him believe his sword had become too painfully hot to hold. He gritted his teeth in anger that he'd fallen for such a childish prank.

Rolling his shoulder, he noted *that* was not a trick. His skin was reddened but not blistered. It had not actually burned, just singed him. He glared at the locked door. It had been more of a force to knock him down rather than set him on fire. Padon spun on his heels and paced the room. How did this demon control such magic?

He growled beneath his breath trying to release his anger. An angry mind gained no ground in a fight. He needed to think clearly. Breathing deep, he did his best to soothe his angst as he sorted his thoughts.

He'd learned from Jasper that three of his *brathairs* were freed from the curse. If his enemy were to be believed, they were headed for a trap and he was the bait. Not if he could help it. His *brathairs* had suffered before because he had failed to kill MacGillivray on that fateful day.

That would not happen again, not now. Not as long as he still breathed.

* * * * *

Lynn fidgeted at the end of the bar. A big floppy straw hat covered her head and she wore a comfortable flowery dress with a pair of sandals. All the items came from a local thrift shop. They took her shopping to buy clothes with a regional flair to help with her disguise. Fin and Travis wanted her to blend in with the regulars at this particular bar in Edinburgh. It's where their little adventure began and where they felt most certain to find Timothy or at least information on his whereabouts.

According to Travis, Timothy's mum hadn't seen him in months and suggested they try the jail or that deadbeat friend of his, Lonnie's place. Now that was a phone call Travis was glad to hang up on. She carried a lot of dislike for her own child. It had him making a promise to visit his own mum as soon as this was over.

Lynn said a silent prayer when she thought of Lonnie. Apparently Thicket MacIntyre's connections through this society to protect Clan MacKinnon ran deep. Three police officers came, collected the body and took care of the situation. Seems Lonnie had a long rap sheet to the point his death wasn't going to draw a huge investigation. The officers moved his body to the apartment he shared with Timothy and claimed they found it there. Since Timothy couldn't be located, he was their number one suspect.

She didn't like they twisted the story, but they did it to protect the society. And to keep her out of an investigation that would probably detain her in Scotland for months. As it was, she had a little over a week left of her vacation and she hoped to spend it with Padon.

If they found him. *Don't think like that,* she told herself as she stared into her cup of tea. They were going to find him. He was alive. She just knew it. Something in her gut gave her hope Padon had not been smashed, that he lingered in his cursed state and at nightfall, he'd awaken. This she believed and the closer it got to dusk the more on edge she became, waiting for that strange tingle down her spine and the electric sizzle in the air she associated with the magic that shattered the stone.

She glanced around. This was where it all started. The pub where Travis spun his tall tale about an ancient ghost in a cave deep within the Grampian Mountains and she believed it. What would've happened if she hadn't believed him? Padon would still be trapped in a stone casket lost in the depths of a cave. She sighed. At least he'd be safe, not stolen like a piece of property and in danger of being smashed to a pulp like he was now. Lynn took a sip of her tea and did her best to calm her nerves. She needed to keep it together if this plan was to work. Unfortunately, it all hinged on Timothy.

Travis and Fin were separated and hidden at opposite corner tables of the bar. If she didn't know they sat there, she wouldn't have seen them due to the low light in those areas and the sizable crowd milling about the place. Oh Lordy, she prayed this worked. If they were right and Timothy was a creature of habit, then he would show up, right? Lynn forced her hand not to shake as she sipped her tea and sat perusing the crowd for any sign of the man.

Out the front window, she saw the last rays of sun dart behind the buildings. Warmth filled her as a familiar sensation sizzled through her. Padon was awake. She sensed it with every fiber of her being. Lynn held her cup with both hands and smiled into it. With him alive, there was hope for finding him or him escaping and returning home on his own. He was strong and she had no doubts that if he escaped, he'd make his way back to a familiar place, Castle MacKinnon. She sat straight with the cup still in her hand as an idea struck.

Did he have to be near for her to feel the strange electricity in the air?

The door opened and time seemed to stop. The crowd disappeared and nothing mattered but the lanky man standing in the doorway. Timothy McFae walked in the place like he owned it.

Lynn tilted her head so the hat's broad brim hid her face. She kept her head at just enough of an angle she could still keep an eye on him in the mirror behind the bar. Not sure if the other two had seen him, she gave them the decided upon signal. She reached her left arm up in a stretching motion and touched a lighted sign. She pressed the button at the bottom and it went out for a second before she turned it on again. Since where Travis sat was in her direct line-of-sight, she saw him slink out of the corner and disappear into the crowd. Without looking to her right, she knew Fin had done the same.

She lowered her gaze when Timothy turned up at her side. Using the hat as her shield, she made sure he couldn't see her face. It didn't appear as if he recognized her when he ordered his drink then turned his back to her and started chatting with the lady on his other side. He was so busy bragging he'd recently come into a huge sum of money he didn't see Travis and Fin box him in.

Travis leaned in on the opposite side of the lady and whispered something dreadful about Timothy in her ear. She gasped, slapped Timothy's face then spun on her heels and left. They knew the moment he regained his focus and realized what had happened. Timothy's eyes widened and his hand dropped from his cheek and automatically became a fist.

"I wouldn't do that," Lynn stretched from the barstool to whisper in Timothy's ear. She pressed something round and solid into the small of his back. "You'd hate it if my finger slipped and made a mess of your back."

He did exactly as she hoped and dropped his hands to his sides. She continued to press the barrel into his back. Fin moved in closer to his side.

"The society would like to have a few words with you," Fin stated staring him down.

"I no longer belong to the society," Timothy proclaimed trying to hold his ground against the three of them, but Lynn heard the fear in his voice.

"You've got that right," Fin snapped. "But we have a way o' dealing with traitors and when we're done, the police want a crack at you for the death o' Lonnie. If there's anything left o' you."

Timothy's Adam's apple bobbed as he swallowed hard. He darted a glance around but no one looked his way.

"That's right," Travis stated calmly. "No one's going to help you. Now let's be walking out the door without any incidences." He nodded toward Lynn. "We wouldn't want the lass to trip and her finger to slip, now would we?"

The moment they exited the bar, a plain white van pulled alongside the curb in front of them. Timothy gasped when the side door slid open and several young men from the society stepped out. They surrounded the group.

"It's okay to put that thing away now, lass," Fin's grandfather said as he worked his way to stand face to face with Timothy.

"Oh, yes," Lynn replied cheerfully. "Just let me do my lips first, they're a bit parched."

Timothy's face fell when he saw she didn't have a gun but a tube of Chap Stick. His cheeks reddened and a fierce snarl rumbled from him as he watched her coat her lips then she tucked it away in the pocket of her sundress.

"Timothy," Thicket MacIntyre stated sternly. "You have but one chance to make an honest man out o' you. Tell us where the MacKinnon be."

"And if'n I don't?" Timothy tilted his chin defiantly and glared directly at Fin's grandfather.

"Then we load you into the van never to be seen again."

The tension in the air made Lynn's skin crawl. She hated confrontation but knew this was unavoidable. The two held their glares locked on one another for what seemed like minutes but wasn't more than a few seconds, before Timothy caved. His decision was helped along by a couple of men in the van obviously rearranging items of torture for him to see. Would they truly use those? Judging from the looks on their faces, she decided they wouldn't hesitate if the need arose.

Nervously, Timothy licked his lips then attempted to make a break for it. He punched at Fin's grandfather, who ducked and landed a solid blow to the younger man's mid-section. Though winded, it didn't stop the freaked-out Timothy. He spun around swinging wildly, hitting anything in his path. Travis grabbed one of Timothy's fists with one hand and punched him in the face with his other hand. His lip split open spurting blood down his chin.

When his loose hand somehow managed to grab a hold of Lynn, she reacted instantly, kicking him in the shin while Travis landed several consecutive blows to his face. Fin clasped Timothy's hand that had a grip on Lynn's shoulder and forced him to release her. Barely able to stand and bleeding profusely from several lacerations on his face and the cut on his lip, Timothy resigned himself to being caught. He spilled his guts and gave them the location of where he'd taken the MacKinnon.

"If this is the money you be boasting all over town about, it will help make peace with your mother," Thicket MacIntyre stated point-blank as he removed the manila envelope from Timothy's inside jacket pocket. Timothy tried to stop him but was held in place by the quick actions of Fin and Travis at his sides.

Thicket turned and got in the passenger seat of the van. The others who had arrived with him returned to the van and shut the door. The three police officers, who'd moved Lonnie's body earlier, had been standing out of sight at the rear of the van waiting for their cue. They moved in to collect Timothy for jail.

"You are under arrest for the murder o' Lonnie Grooms," one of them said as he moved to stand face to face with Timothy. One of the other two pulled his hands behind his back and locked his wrists in handcuffs. The third one read him his rights as they shoved him into the back of a police van that pulled in behind the society's van.

Travis and Fin spoke briefly with Thicket MacIntyre and laid out a plan of action. They would meet at the piers in South Queensbury. There were several that were no longer used for ferry services. Timothy hadn't been specific as to which one housed the MacKinnon and Brother Leod's hideout. Though they wanted to leave Lynn behind, she refused and hopped into the back seat of Fin's sedan.

The early evening traffic wasn't too congested so they made good time. They parked behind an active food market down the street from one of the unused ferry locations. Though the ferry services no longer ran, the area still maintained a mini-mall, a few scattered houses and an apartment building on the main road before the turnoff for the street that led to the piers. With three possibilities to choose from, they split into teams and made their way in different directions away from the community. A few feet from the building she, Travis and Fin were assigned to, Lynn stopped dead still.

"He's not in this one," she whispered and closed her eyes as if concentrating all her senses on just one thing — Padon.

A tingle started in her core and trickled outward to the tips of her toes, her fingers and her nose. She shivered, opening her eyes. "I know where he is."

She turned and took deliberate steps toward the worst of the old ferry piers. She kept her flashlight pointed downward and hoped the tall grass helped hide her movements from anyone who may be inside the run-down building located on the far end of the pier. Sneaking up on them would be impossible since they had to traverse the length of the rickety wooden structure to get to them. Travis and Fin followed after giving the birdcall signal to the others.

Once they'd all gathered in the overgrown weeds, several of the stealthier young men were assigned to swim along the pilings under the pier and climb up to flank the building from the far end. When they were in position, they were to give the signal and the others would attempt to sneak along the pier to the building.

Lynn closed her eyes and said a silent prayer.

Please keep Padon and these men safe. Don't you think being cursed for two hundred years was enough trouble for this family?

Her prayer was cut off and their actions stalled when two cars turned down the lane that led to the pier. Everyone ducked close to the ground until the cars had passed. They watched as the cars came to a stop and parked near the pier they had intended to search. Everyone kept hidden but all eyes remained on the individuals getting out of the cars. Five people in total, a man and a woman who drove the cars and three rather large men got out of the passenger seats.

They were too far away to hear the words that were exchanged. From her body language, the woman wasn't happy at having to stay behind. One of the big guys picked her up and sat her on the hood of the car she had driven then he kissed her on the forehead. The smaller of the men remained with the woman as the other three walked down the pier toward the building. They disappeared inside when the door was opened.

Damn. This couldn't be good. Lynn chewed her bottom lip and waited. Travis and Thicket sat on each side of her while the younger men did as they were instructed. They moved without being seen by the man or the woman as they entered the water, using the weeds and overgrowth as their cover.

Lynn noted Thicket stared at the man and the woman left behind at the cars. Was he plotting a way to deal with them? After several long seconds, he leaned close to her and Travis.

"This may not be as bad as it seems."

Without further comment, he stood and walked toward the cars. The man took a fighting stance as the woman scrambled from the hood, grabbed a heavy-looking stick from the driver's seat through the open window and made ready to use it.

Had Thicket lost his mind? He was going to get the shit beat out of him.

Chapter Twelve

Padon carefully walked around the room, taking note of which floorboards creaked, which didn't and which seemed to sink with his weight. With every pass of the wind, the room swayed making him aware of the delicate condition of the building. He shut off the light the way Lynn had shown him at the MacIntyres' farmhouse. Beams of moonlight streamed in through assorted cracks in the ceiling. He moved into the far corner of the room and looked out of that window hoping to obtain a different perspective on his location if possible.

From this angle, he saw he was out over the water in a stilted abode at the end of some sort of walkway. He caught sight of several dark people-shaped dots moving into the water from the shoreline. Someone was swimming and disappeared out of view underneath the walkway. Who and why? He squinted letting his eyes adjust to the darkness both inside and outside of the window. Movements in the weeds gave him proof whoever was in the water was not alone.

If he saw them, it was a great possibility so did Brother Leod and his men. How many men were in Leod's band of disciples? If they were all like the few he'd encountered already—Lonnie, Timothy and the big redhead—then escape would not be an issue. The problem he now faced were those in the water and along the shore. Who were they and what did they want? He removed the curtain from the window so his view would not be obscured then he went to work on a weakened floorboard.

He wedged the tip of the sword between two of the rotted planks. It didn't take much to pry it loose. The edges of the board crumbled as he worked it free as silently as possible. When he managed to remove the third board, he caught sight of a person looking up at him from the water.

"MacKinnon, it be good to see you again," the male voice stated in a hushed tone but loud enough for him to hear it.

Padon grinned. "It be good to see ya again as well, Fin."

He reached down and gave him a hand up through the hole in the floor. Once secure inside, Fin lay on his stomach with his head inside the hole and spoke to someone Padon couldn't see.

"Let them know, we've found him." A second later he was in a crouched position at

Padon's side. "Any idea how many we're up against on the inside?"

"Nay," Padon answered keeping his voice low. If the building swayed in the wind, he didn't doubt the walls were thin and any noise may be heard easily if they weren't careful. "To my knowledge there be only two but I doubt that be all o' them."

"It's not. We saw three more enter the building so that makes at least five. No telling how many more may be here already. Can you swim?"

"Aye," Padon replied with a nod. "The hole need be larger for me to fit."

Before Fin could help pull more boards from around the hole, Padon caught him by the arm. With a finger to his lips, he nodded toward the door. Male voices could faintly be heard coming down the hall. Heavy footfalls came closer and closer. Quickly, he and Fin lifted the old desk that was already turned over and set it in front of the hole. Since it wasn't far from where the desk was to begin with, he hoped it wouldn't be noticed they'd moved it. Fin ducked behind the desk making sure the removed floorboards were out of sight as well.

Padon took long strides placing distance between him and his escape route hoping not to draw attention to it or Fin. He drew his sword and stood ready for another mini-skirmish for his freedom. A sideways grin tickled his lips at the thought of another fight. Aye, it had been way too long since he'd had a decent fight to blow off the tension pent-up frustration built within him. He licked his lips as Lynn's face popped into his head for a second and reminded him he was frustrated in more ways than one. The heaviness within his bawls wouldn't let him forget it.

He spun his sword in his hands and readied himself for the only relief he was going to get anytime soon. Let's just hope this one was more o' a challenge than the last. He sighed.

The door swung opened and a nasally voice announced, "As promised," right before a thin man wearing glasses let go of the door knob and stepped back into the hall out of sight.

Though he couldn't see him, Padon recognized the next voice instantly. "You best nay be lying or you be paying with your tongue."

The grin couldn't be stopped as the words of his *brathair*, Ian, tickled his ears as well as his heart. It was a voice he believed he'd never hear again. His eyes widened with joy as his oldest *brathair*, Gavin entered the room.

"Padon!" Gavin's happiness resounded in his one word exclamation as he closed the distance between them. Padon sheathed his sword right before they hugged tight. He didn't want to let go for fear it was all a dream and Gavin would vanish.

"It be good to see you, Padon." He heard another of his *brathair's* voice. Struan.

He opened his eyes as he pushed out of Gavin's hug. Ian and Struan stood behind Gavin. Each clasped him tight, patting his back and claiming their joy at his return home.

"But you are not home," Brother Leod's sinister tone stated from the doorway, "and you never will be."

Ian and Struan both lunged in his direction but he was well calculated in his move, slamming and locking the door closed. Ian pressed his ear to the door and listened. After a few seconds, he turned back to them.

"It sounded to be three sets o' feet. The sniveling wimp who led us here, MacGillivray and another heavier person." He shrugged with a grin. "Probably that idiot he calls his right hand, Roy."

"A redhead, meaty kind o' guy with limited wits," Padon asked.

"Aye." Ian nodded.

"Then that be him." He turned toward the desk. "It be clear, Fin." When he stood, Padon introduced him. "This be Fin MacIntyre. He be here to help."

"MacIntyre?" Gavin stated the question as if he were thinking of something or someone. "You be kin to Thicket MacIntyre?"

"You know his name?" Fin sounded surprised as he nodded. "Most just call him Ol' Man Thicket."

"I nay be like most." Gavin grinned.

"Aye, that be the truth," Padon, Ian and Struan stated in unison then the *brathairs* laughed.

Padon cleared his throat and his voice took a somber tone. "I be afraid you have fallen into a trap at my expense."

"We expected it," Struan piped in with a smile upon his face.

"This Brother Leod has some sort o' magical control over fire," Padon replied on a rushed breath. He needed his *brathairs* to know what he'd learned of their enemy.

"We know. It nay be a good resource for him," Ian said with a bit of humor in his voice. "How do you think he lost his good looks the last time we met? You think he would learn not to mess with the MacKinnon *brathairs*."

The knot in Padon's chest relaxed. His *brathairs* knew it was a trap and still came. They came for him, even though he had not succeeded in killing MacGillivray and prevented them from being cursed. Instead he had fallen as well. This blasted curse may have kept them separated, suspended in time for many years but it had not broken their tight-knit bond as *brathairs*.

He breathed more easily, knowing the curse could and would be defeated. The MacKinnon *brathairs* would make sure of it. Vengeance would be sought if it meant his last breath in the name of his family. He swallowed deep preventing the monster of hatred to rear its ugly head and mar his reunion. There would be time for the hunt for MacGillivray and a time to kill that black-hearted demon.

"I hate to cut this reunion short," Fin interrupted. "I smell kerosene. We need to be leav—" He didn't get to finish the sentence before flames started licking the walls.

Gavin attempted to grab the doorknob but it was too hot and sealed shut by the locks.

"This way, *brathairs*. We have a way out," Padon announced as he shoved the desk across the room showing the hole in the floor.

Since he no longer needed to worry about silence, he grabbed another board and yanked it from the edge of the hole. It had to be several feet wider if he and his *brathairs* were to fit. Ian grabbed a board from the other side and pulled it free. The walls around them ignited into flames urging them to work quicker. Everyone grabbed floor planks, tugging and ripping them loose, tossing them aimlessly at the flames as if it would slow its hungry progress by being content to devour their puny offering of rotted wood.

The second the hole was big enough for all to fit, Fin lowered through followed by Straun. Ian hesitated.

"You know I hate to be wet unless it be inside Izzy," he jested.

Gavin glanced around at the fire swallowing the room and shoved him hard. "Wet and safe or dry and burned to a crisp. The latter you never be between Izzy's thighs again."

"Point taken." Ian dropped and landed with a splash, sending water up through the hole with the force of a geyser.

Boards cracked around them as the fire grew. Neither waited. Gavin quickly followed Padon into the water. It seemed as if they barely hit the water before the walls of the room caved in. The only things keeping the building from falling in on top of them was the solid underpinning and pilings, but it was a matter of time before those were engulfed as well.

"Padon," Lynn screamed as she ran toward the burning building. Travis caught her around the waist and snatched her from her feet holding her tight against him. He dragged her away from the pier's edge.

"Lass, you can't go out there. It's not safe." As if to emphasize his words, the building crumbled upon itself and the pier became engulfed in flames. "Damn. Fin."

She heard his muttered words and knew he was worried for Fin's safety as was she once it hit her Fin was out there as well as several others. She stopped struggling and leaned into him giving as much as receiving support as they waited, hoping for a miracle.

The woman she had just met named Izzy stood at her side staring out over the water. She twisted a section of her shoulder-length, two-toned colored hair in her fingers nervously as she waited. The top section of her hair was dark but about two inches of it from the end was bright white as if she were letting it grow out to its natural color. The way the fire danced in her brilliant green eyes made them appear as if they were glowing with anger mixed with despair and she chewed her lower lip intently showing her angst. Lynn reached and touched her shoulder, giving her a weak smile of hope. Izzy only nodded, battling back tears that threatened to fall at any second.

Ned stood beside her and Lynn saw the pain in his face. The older man maintained a stocky fighter's stance and didn't say much. But it was obvious. He was more than a member of the society. She'd learned a few minutes earlier he worked for a woman named May, who came from America in search of a castle and a family who'd been cursed. In her heart, she believed in the story she'd read in an old diary she'd found in a box of books at a store going out of business. It turned out to be the MacKinnon brothers' sister, Akira's, diary. According to Ned, if it weren't for May's strong will and tenacity, the brothers would probably never have been found and freed.

"Ian, you best be safe," Izzy stated as if voicing her wishes made them happen.

"I be nothing less, my *dona leannan.*" Squealing, she turned and ran toward the dark figure walking from the water off to the right of the burning pier. When she leapt, he caught her in his arms and kissed her so passionately, Lynn blushed. There was no doubt those two were a pair and belonged to one another.

Looking past the ardent couple, Lynn's heart pounded at the sight of Padon taking long hurried strides in her direction. His flesh was cold and wet when he took her in his arms. Water dripped from his hair but she didn't care. He was safe.

"I thought you were trapped inside." She looked toward what was left of the burning pier. His fingers touched her chin and turned her face to him.

"A madman and his fire can nay keep me from ye, my wee one." Padon captured her lips and led her mouth into the hottest kiss she ever remembered.

Lifting onto the balls of her feet, she deepened the kiss not caring who watched or stood near. She stretched her arms around his neck as best as possible. His hands moved to her back tugging her tightly against him. The wet kilt around his waist did nothing to hide the way he felt about her. His hardness pressed against her abdomen and as short as she was, it seemed to poke her in the belly button.

"Ahem." Travis cleared his throat loudly to gain their attention. It thrilled her to see Fin stood safely at his side with Travis' arm hanging loosely across his shoulders. When they broke apart, he added quickly nodding his head toward the sound of sirens far off in the distance. "We need to be leaving or we may have a lot to answer for."

Padon brushed another quick kiss to her lips. "Until later, my wee one." The heat in his eyes promised more than just a kiss and her stomach did flips.

They turned in unison to see Ian at the water's edge with a bow and arrow.

"You say you saw a boat tied under the pier and you undid the plug for the fuel." He was talking to one of the men who had swum under the pier with Fin to rescue Padon.

"Aye," the young man proclaimed excitedly as he pointed at a dot on the water headed upriver. "It was draining as they boarded so it shouldn't last much longer before they run out o' fuel."

Ian wrapped something tightly around the tip of his arrow then dipped it in the fire that was devouring the end of the pier.

"Ian, we need to go before they get here," Gavin pointed out sternly as he held one of the car doors opened.

The others were already in their respective cars with the exception of the man, who stood beside Ian. Struan stood behind Gavin watching Ian. Padon stopped to watch his *brathair*, but didn't let go of Lynn's hand as they stood beside the car Gavin had told them to get in. Ned sat behind the wheel with the car running and ready to go. Lynn smiled at Ned when he leaned out the window and yelled.

"Hurry up, lad, and be done with 'em. We don't have all night. I be needing me a stiff one."

"As do I, *m'cariad*," Ian called out as he winked at Izzy then positioned the arrow in the bowstring. Izzy grinned and slid into the driver's seat of her car. Lynn felt heat in her cheeks again at the blatant meaning in his words and his actions. She couldn't stop the tingle in her nipples at the hope of being alone with Padon later, *if* she were lucky.

Ian aimed at the dot that seemed to have now stalled on the water about a hundred yards out. It appeared to her as if it were an impossible shot. She held her breath as the arrow flew straight and true. It didn't miss. The boat lit up like a bonfire. Screams echoed across the water but they couldn't tell from that distance if anyone dove overboard.

Ian spun on his heels and ran toward Izzy's waiting car as he shouted to the man running beside him. "You were right. You did get some o' the fuel 'n the boat."

Chapter Thirteen

It seemed like a whirlwind captured her and spun her around for the rest of the night. It took them several hours to travel to Castle MacKinnon where Gavin's wife, Ericka, greeted them at the door. Gavin hugged her as if he hadn't seen her for days even though it had only been a matter of hours. When he turned to introduce her, it was obvious she was pregnant. Standing behind her with his arm protectively around her waist and his hand on her belly, Gavin introduced her to his brother.

"Padon, this is my wife, Ericka." He grinned as he rubbed her tummy. "And this be our child."

Red graced Ericka's cheeks and Lynn thought that was adorable. Even though she knew her husband intimately, she still blushed. Padon took a knee at Ericka's feet and fisted his hand over his heart.

"I vow to protect the new lady o' Castle MacKinnon with my life." A knot formed in Lynn's throat at the conviction in his voice.

The petite auburn-haired beauty cupped Padon's cheek. "Welcome home, Padon. I appreciate your honorable gift. Things are different now. We live here together as one big happy family. No one rules the other. If anyone is head of this household, it's Aunt May." She smiled and her green eyes seemed to brighten behind her glasses. "I'm sure she's going to love hearing you're home safe." She looked past Padon and said, "Please come in. I'm sure you're all probably hungry and I know a couple of people who'd love to hear your tale."

"That be a mighty fine offer, Ericka," Thicket MacIntyre replied. "But the society be having an emergency meeting at Grant's Tavern. We just wanted to see him safely home before leaving." He nodded.

Travis handed Lynn her rental car keys. "I'll come by tomorrow with your things. I take it you'll be staying here?" He directed the question at Padon instead of Lynn.

Lynn didn't get the chance to answer. Padon held his hand out to Travis. "Thank ye, *m'cariad*. Lynn be staying here for as long as she likes." He turned to Fin and shook his hand as well.

She hugged Travis first. His whispered words caught her off-guard but warmed her heart. "I thank you for all you've done for me. Without your help, I'd still be living a nightmare cursed by a haunted laird."

He pressed a kiss to her cheek and heat skittered up her neck to her face. Lynn cupped his cheek. "It is I who thank you. It was you who took me on an adventure of a lifetime and gave me the sweetest reward of all. Friendship."

Travis took her hands in his. "Lass, having you as my friend is golden." He hugged her tight then released her and walked toward the waiting van.

Fin gave her a tight hug.

"Thank you for everything," Lynn said. "I'll see you both, tomorrow."

"You can count on it." Fin grinned then whispered low so only she would hear, "You are a perfect match for the MacKinnon, my friend. Let the heart guide you and your spirit shall be free." With a wink, he turned and headed for the van.

Lynn couldn't help but smile at his beautiful words. Those two were a magnificent couple. Both were strong characters with hearts of pure gold and she wouldn't trade anything for their friendship. Was Fin right? Was she a perfect match for Padon?

After the men left, Ericka led them into the castle. Lynn couldn't help but stop and admire a huge tapestry that hung in the main hallway. Seven brothers stood behind two women who sat on a bench in a garden. Each of the men bore resemblances to one another and varied in heights and ages. It took her no time to recognize Padon. He was the most handsome of all as far as she was concerned.

The heat of his breath near her ear sent a chill down her neck as he spoke. "That be my family many years ago." He pointed out Gavin, Ian and Struan whom she recognized. The other three she didn't know. Aiden and the twins, Donnell and Dour, were still missing. Their statues had not been located. She sighed sadly.

Padon's fingers touched her chin and she met his eyes. Determination shone within them and sounded in his tone. "Don't ye worry, my wee one. We shall find them and bring them home."

"Glad you feel that way my *brathair*," Ian said as he clamped a hand down on Padon's shoulder. "Step into the library and we shall catch you up on the hunt for the others."

They walked through the doorway and entered one of the most beautiful libraries she'd ever seen in a person's home. Come to think of it, it was the only library she'd ever seen inside a home. Three walls were lined with shelves of books. On one of those walls, a gorgeous fireplace was in the center and separated the bookshelves. The fourth wall was filled with windows and a set of double doors. In the middle of the room were two couches facing each other with a large coffee table between them. On either end of the coffee table sat large winged-back chairs that matched the leather couches.

Several stands with dry-erase boards and assorted other items were placed about the room. Two tables sat on the opposite side of the room with a couple of stacks of books and notepads on them. A huge map hung from a stand in front of one of the bookshelves. Stickpins dotted it with color. It was obvious to Lynn this was the room where they gathered to search for the missing brothers.

Struan introduced a gorgeous woman named Caledonia as his fiancée. She had long jet-black hair pulled in a ponytail and the oddest color of blue eyes Lynn had ever seen. A short round woman with gray hair came into the room carrying a tray of goodies. Ericka introduced her as Margaret who worked as the housekeeper of the castle and was married to Ned. Lynn really liked Margaret's motherly attitude as she swept about the room making everyone comfortable.

A flash of light beamed into the room. An ethereal beauty floated in front of Padon. Long red hair flowed to her waist and brilliant green eyes stared from a face of pure porcelain. When she spoke, her voice was soft and her brogue had an alluring lilt.

"It be good to see ye home, Padon."

"My *brathairs* told me ye be a ghost, my *piuthar*, but it took seeing ye with my own eyes to believe it." Tears shimmered in his eyes and Lynn's heart melted. It had to hurt him to see his only sister as a ghost.

"Nay, don't ye shed a tear for me, Padon." Her transparent hand cupped Padon's cheek and she smiled. "I have waited a long time for ye to return. It be time to celebrate, not linger in thy past over things that cannot be changed. We have three more to find and free. Are ye with us?"

"Aye," Padon stated clearly without hesitation. "I be with ye for eternity, my *piuthar*."

"And who be this lovely lady?" Akira asked as she floated to face Lynn.

"She be my wee one, Lynn Woodberry o' Texas," Padon answered as he stepped to Lynn's side. "Lynn, this be my *piuthar*, Akira."

Meeting Akira had Lynn bursting internally with questions, but she chose to be polite and hold off on her inquiry about the afterlife until another time. Tonight was about Padon reuniting with his family. She couldn't help but notice Akira's eyebrow arched when he called her his wee one. She wasn't even sure if Padon realized he did it.

"It's nice to meet you, Akira," Lynn said politely.

"And ye as well. Lynn, ye are welcome. Please sit. We have so much to learn o' how Padon was released." Akira smiled and Lynn relaxed, but not completely.

She noted Akira shot the other women in the room a knowing gaze they seemed to return. What was that about? Were they making fun of her somehow and if so why? What had she done? Lynn shook off the overactive thoughts and tossed them aside as being too tired to think clearly. These women weren't making fun of her. She tried to convince herself, but something hinted they were up to something so she decided she'd cautiously watch and see if it happened again.

She took a seat on the couch beside Ericka. Unfortunately, May was not home. She was in London following a lead for what she hoped were the missing twins' statues.

From what she'd heard of this Aunt May from Gavin and Struan on the ride to the castle, the woman was worth meeting and spending time getting to know. Lynn hoped she got the opportunity before she had to return to Texas. In the world of spiritual dalliances, Aunt May seemed to be an expert and it would be a shame not to speak with her.

Lynn found it odd that whenever she or Padon mentioned the curse and how to break it completely, no one gave them a straight answer. Or if they had, maybe she was simply too exhausted to comprehend it from their cryptic clues. They seemed so nice and welcoming she was certain she misunderstood their evasiveness as a tiny matter of trust for her. After all, they'd just met. They really didn't know her. Maybe once they did, things would change. If not, then hopefully they'd at least tell Padon.

Several times throughout the evening, she noted the "look" passed between the women and it weighed on her frayed nerves. Lynn breathed deep and tried desperately to convince herself that she'd imagined the "look" but a little voice inside her dug in planting a seed something was going on, no matter what she wanted to believe.

She sat back, focused on the brothers and enjoyed the sibling rivalry between them and let them squash her suspicions. They made her laugh and soon she forgot all about the strange "look" she thought had occurred between the women. Love and family togetherness filled the room and warmed her to her toes. This was something she missed. With her sister's family, she knew she was loved and a big part of their lives, but when she returned home from her visits with them, she was very much alone. Lynn breathed deep determined not to dwell on herself. This was Padon's homecoming.

Besides, she'd called her sister when she arrived and filled her in on the minor details leaving out much of the story—the kidnapping, the almost falling to her death, the finding a ghost and then partially freeing a two hundred-plus-year old man from an ancient curse. That was a tale she needed to tell in person. As far as her sister was concerned, she was staying at a castle with a group of wonderful people for the rest of her visit. It had been enough to satisfy her sister and halt her concerns about not being able to contact her over the last few days.

For the rest of the evening, she let Padon's family entertain her with stories of their youth. It was easier to relax and let go when the "look" stopped or at least she didn't notice it anymore. Margaret kept the nibbles and drinks flowing until everyone was full. A few hours before daybreak, Padon took Lynn's hand as they disbanded for the evening.

He led her to his wing of the castle. The beauty of the castle astounded her. Once they ascended the staircase and entered the sitting room of his tower, he stopped, pulled her into his arms and kissed her.

"I have been waiting to do that all night," he whispered against her lips.

"Me too," Lynn replied. She couldn't look anywhere but Padon's gorgeous gaze. Lust heated the air between them.

Padon scooped her into his arms and strode directly into the bedchamber. An overly large bed sat across the room. The ornately carved headboard seemed to cover most of that wall. A thick white eyelet blanket covered the bed and matching pillows leaned against the headboard. His eyebrow arched as he looked around.

"Seems a woman hath decorated since my last rest 'n my bedchamber."

Lynn laughed. "I like it. It's pretty."

"It be womanly." Padon huffed. She noted he rubbed his feet in the carpet, staring down at it as if it were a foreign substance.

She laid her palm against his cheek and turned his attention back to her. "Do you want to learn about the décor or enjoy your last few hours of this night in my arms on that bed?"

His face split with a great big grin. "I like the way my wee one thinks."

When he headed toward the bed, she redirected him to an open door off to the left of the room. His brows pursed but he did as she suggested. Once he entered the bathroom she had him put her down. She kicked off her sandals leaving them by the door. He stood staring in wonder at the room, but held his questions when she turned to face him and reached for his kilt.

She smiled as she tackled the task of removing his kilt, which was still slightly damp from his earlier swim. She tsked at him. "Why didn't you change out of this wet thing?"

He shrugged as he stood still watching her undress him. He toyed with a tangle of curls brushing them from her eyes. "It no bothered me."

"Well, you won't be needing it tonight." She loosened it and wiggled it free of his hips, letting it glide down his legs to pool at his feet.

It didn't surprise her Padon was true to his kilt. Though she hadn't actually noticed anything but him once he'd undressed before entering the waterfall, she wasn't sure until now he wore not a stitch of clothing beneath it. He stood proud for her inspection but she couldn't move. Naked he was the most amazing man she'd ever seen. Strength flowed seamlessly through every muscle, every well-defined line from his chest and shoulders all the way down his abdomen and legs to his toes and seemed to culminate along one phenomenal pinnacle of male anatomy.

Padon took her hands in his, lifted them to his lips then kissed the insides of each of her wrists. The delicate touch of his kisses was extremely sensual sending heat coursing through her. The look in his eyes stole her breath. Promises of pleasure danced in those deep blue-greens igniting a fire of need in her core that only he could extinguish.

"Seems I'm the only one naked. We need to rectify that."

Lynn couldn't speak as he deftly removed her sundress tugging it up from the waist and off over her head and arms. His brows pursed at the sight of her bra but his eyes glowed with curiosity mixed with pure desire. Ever so lightly, his fingertips traced the lace cupping her healthy bosoms. She reached behind her back and unhooked the clasps, loving the instant response of wonder in his face as he caught the bra and slid it from her arms. It was like it was Christmas and she was his present to unwrap.

He held it to his nose and audibly inhaled. His ardent gaze never left hers. "This be an item I envy."

"Why?" croaked from Lynn's lips. Her mouth didn't want to function properly under his hungry-eyed scrutiny. He looked as if he'd devour her at any moment and in his case, she wouldn't mind one bit.

He dropped the bra and cupped her bare breasts in his hands. "Ye are heartily blessed, my wee one. Would be wonderful to caress them all day as my sole purpose for existing."

Padon thumbed her nipples gently while his gaze held hers. In slow motion, he lowered to capture one taut bud between his lips. Lynn's knees wobbled but she managed to remain standing. He lavished her nipple tenderly suckling while his hands massaged both breasts. The thumb of the one hand worked her other nipple into a hard point. Lynn clung to his arms for support. The more he loved her breasts the weaker her knees became. His actions had her turned on, hot and wet, ready for more than his touch.

Lynn dropped her hand to his erection and Padon froze. His eyes opened wide. She read the desire in his gaze as if it were written on a bright neon sign saying this way to ecstasy. She swallowed the laugh that threatened at the silly thought and ruled it as nerves. Padon was the hottest, sexiest man she'd ever wanted to be with and it was obvious from the solid length of him in her hand the feeling was mutual.

Delicately she ran her open palm along the velvety soft skin stretched to capacity along hardened steel. He moaned when she cupped his balls and his thumbs rewarded her nipples by circling them in a sensual caress, which made her tremble. Damn, this was killing her, but she wanted this to be an experience neither of them would ever forget. At least that's what she hoped. Lynn shook off the nervous twitter forming in her gut and released him. She abruptly turned and moved to the tub.

"I want to take a shower," she said.

She started the water, tested the temperature until it was comfortable then switched it to the shower. Lynn faced Padon with a big smile as she slid her panties down her legs and stepped out of them. "You want to join me?"

Standing naked in front of him, her insides knotted and she couldn't breathe as she awaited his approval.

He licked his lips hungrily as he shook his head. "Thy wish is my command, my wee one."

Padon's jaw went slack and it was all he could do not to let his tongue loll out of his mouth like a dog at the wondrous sight of Lynn in all of her glory. She was beyond beautiful. From the tip of her pert little nose to the spiked nipples of her heavy breasts down her smooth abdomen to her hairless mound. His eyes widened at the sight of no hair between her thighs. Sex in the waterfall had been so hard and fast that he did not remember the fact her mound was smooth. Was she born that way or did she strive to keep it that clean? *Och*, his heart pounded heartily within the walls of his chest.

He took her hand and kissed her wrists, then slid his hands along her arms to her shoulders, down her back to cup the soft round globes of her arse. He wanted to keep touching her and never stop. Womanly curves in all the right places.

"My wee one, ye are truly a magnificent woman," rasped from his lips right before he captured her mouth in a tender kiss. Padon lifted her in his arms and stepped into the tub.

Refreshingly warm water sprayed them from a round object hanging from the wall. For a split second, he stared at it until Lynn kissed him returning his attention to her. She slid down his body turning him on at every brush of skin on skin. Her nipples touched his sending a bolt of need to tighten his bawls. Even though she was much shorter than he, she was perfect for him.

When her feet touched down, she grabbed a bar of soap and lathered his chest. This was the first time a woman had ever bathed him since he was a *bairn*. If he remembered correctly, he fought those, but this one was different. The trail of her hands and lavender-scented foam set his skin aflame. He wanted her never to stop when she gathered his shaft and bawls in her delicate hands and washed him as if he were a precious prize. It took every ounce of inner strength he could muster not to expend himself in her hands. He swallowed hard then captured her wrists, tenderly tugging her hands free.

He lowered until his forehead touched hers and their gazes met. "If ye continue to lavish me with such wonderful attention, I fear I shall be spent. 'Tis not how I wish this evening to go."

Lynn turned him to face the water and helped rinse off the suds. Her hands on his back sent a tingle down his spine and soothed any ache his muscles may have had. The way she washed him had him on fire with need to be buried within her heat. Never had he felt so hard to the point he thought it might break should he bump it against something. He lifted his face into the steady stream struggling for control. Her pleasure was first and foremost his top concern. When she urged him to face her, he doubted he'd last if she touched him again.

Padon grasped the soap from her before she could place it back in its holder. "My turn, my wee one."

The hoarseness in which his words were spoken surprised him. Her beautiful ways not only had him hard and hungry for her but made it difficult for him to speak as well. *Och,* what magic had she weaved upon him? Feeling the fullness of her breasts in his palms as he washed them whisked away that thought. He truly cared not if she'd cast a spell upon him, especially if it meant he got to spend time with her, caressing every inch of her beautiful body.

Slowly he lowered to his knees, washing and rinsing her flesh. The sight of her nipples protruding through a trail of suds made him smile at the sudden thought of snowcapped mountains. He stretched upward and nipped a tender bud playfully, which rewarded him with a sensual moan from somewhere deep inside her throat. The sound nearly undid his resolve to taste her before he entered her. Padon shuddered inwardly grappling for the reins on his lust before it galloped away from him.

"Do ye trust me, wee one?" he asked as he looked into her eyes. Her nod was all he needed to feast upon her treasure.

He ran a finger along her sheath and loved the silken feel. Hot and wet, ready for him. Padon couldn't resist. He stooped lower and licked between her folds delving his tongue in search of the tender bud he knew was hidden. Finding it, he suckled and licked until a moan careened from her. He inserted a finger into her heat, pumping in rhythm to the motion of his tongue and lips. Her knees buckled and he managed to keep her standing until he'd lapped her clean of her juices.

Padon stood, taking her in his arms. He tilted her face and smiled. "My wee one, ye are sweeter than any nectar. I could drink forever and never be full."

He kissed her, sharing her taste with her and loved the passionate response she gave him. Tongue upon tongue lavished each other with wants and desires increasing their hunger for each other. Lynn let go of him long enough to turn off the water. She led him from the shower. When she reached for a pair of towels, he ravished her rump with a playful nip to each exquisite mound.

She jumped and squealed. He laughed. "I like a fine behind on a lass and ye have a beautiful one."

Without giving her a chance to dry off, he scooped her into his arms and hurried to the bed. Not caring about the covers, he laid her on the bed and landed at her side. Padon kissed her, taking in as much of her as he could. His fingers parted her folds and made her ready for him. The urge to be inside her overwhelmed him and he couldn't wait any longer. Padon moved and she spread her legs beckoning him between them. He paused for a second taking in the essence and glory that was his wee one.

The most gorgeous woman he'd ever seen, lay waiting for him to make love with her. Pink, wet and perfect went through his head as he positioned his shaft at her entrance. Never had he wanted to take his time in pleasing a woman. This was different and he knew it. He could spend an eternity between her thighs and never get enough.

Padon pushed in slowly, rejoicing in the feel of her accepting him. Her legs tightened around him tugging him in deeper. Heaven couldn't compare to the woman beneath him. Once he was fully seated, he stopped, letting her relax around him. Then he slid until the head of his shaft lingered within her opening then plunged bawl deep again. Her sighs of pleasure urged him on. Her heeling him in the back of the thighs increased his pace.

"Padon," she gasped as she arched off the bed taking him to her deepest point. "Please! I need more of you."

He halted all motion as he kissed her. Her whispered plea of please against his lips broke his restraint to love her easily this time. Her nails clawed at his back as he did as she requested. The pace she set was fast and hard and he refused to fail at pleasing Lynn. He nuzzled her neck and inched along her sensitive skin to suckle from nipple to nipple. When he took more of her breast into his mouth, she gasped and bucked. Her inner muscles clenched him tightly and he lost control.

He let go of her breasts and groaned as his seed released deep within her heat. The entire length of him throbbed as her sheath massaged him into submission. Their juices combined cascading around him as he lay nestled within her. Nay, heaven could not be better than being in Lynn's arms and buried within her treasure.

Padon collapsed onto his side taking her with him. Keeping her cocooned close, he managed to stay inside her heat, a place he never wanted to leave. Out of the corner of his eye, he noted the change in the color of the sky and knew their time was limited. It wouldn't be much longer and he'd have to separate from her and wait until the fall of the sun to hold her once again. He sighed against her neck, then kissed her earlobe as he held her tight.

Lynn didn't want to move. Padon had given her some of the best sex of her life. He lavished her breasts as if he'd secretly known she loved having them touched and sucked during sex. It kept her hot and bothered and each time his teeth nipped the over-sensitive nipple a sharp spike of need bolted straight to her core. She trembled inside just thinking about it.

Though she loved the feel of him inside her, wrapped around her, she knew from the clock on the nightstand morning would soon be upon them. Regretfully, she'd have to move when the curse took him from her again. Sadness filled her heart. Lynn closed her eyes tight and had to swallow hard not to cry.

A sudden chill brushed her face as if something ice cold touched her cheek. Lynn's eyes opened wide and her heart skipped a beat at the sight.

Eddie stood in the open doorway to the balcony. He beckoned for her to join him. Heat filled her cheeks and she knew her face must be every shade of red possible. Her husband stood on the balcony looking straight at her as she lay naked in the arms of another man. From their position, there was no hiding they'd just had sex. Oh God, she was going to hell.

"You're not going to hell, Lynn," Eddie's voice said with a laugh. "Come visit with me. I only have a few moments."

Lynn sat up and looked at Padon. It appeared as if he slept. Glancing at the clock, it seemed as if time stood still. The second hand no longer ticked. She looked at Eddie with her brows pursed, not sure if she were dreaming.

"I've stopped time for a few moments so we can talk, but I can't do it for long."

She nodded as if hearing it from him made it okay and believable. Quietly, she stood, gathered the forgotten towel from the floor, wrapped it around her then slowly walked out onto the balcony. The early morning sky seemed held frozen threatening to sport the sun at any given moment. Usually she found the colors beautiful but today they were her enemy. It meant Padon's curse lingered on the horizon waiting to capture him at first light.

"Eddie, I—" He didn't give her a chance to explain herself or how she'd ended up in bed with another man. Shame had her stomach in a knot and her heart hurting with indecision. Even though Eddie was dead, guilt bloomed like a weed trying to take over and strangle her happiness.

He touched her cheek and an icy sensation coated her skin but she didn't flinch. This was Eddie. Though he was transparent, he was still her husband. She met his gaze with tears in her eyes.

"Lynn, no matter what you think, you haven't cheated on me." He thumbed her tears away. A big grin split his face and his eyes lit up like they always had when he smiled. "I'm dead."

She shook her head. "That's a pretty cold way of saying it." She couldn't help smiling back at him.

"It's the truth. Besides, you know how I feel about sex, keep it spontaneous, go with the flow and enjoy every moment. That's exactly what you did in the waterfall."

Lynn's cheeks heated even more and her eyes widened. "You saw that?"

Eddie grinned. "Don't worry. I watched only long enough to make sure he had no intention of hurting you then I left." He wagged his eyebrows at her. "I trust you had a great time?"

An unstoppable smile crossed her lips and Lynn couldn't help but answer. "Yes. It was amazing."

"That's what I'd hoped. I know it was the first time you had sex since my death." He touched her cheek and the tender look in his eyes eased her discomfort. This was Eddie. This was her late husband so talking about sex was okay and felt right to her. "Lynn, you are a vibrant, beautiful woman and you deserve happiness. Take it. Maybe he can give you the one thing I never could."

Her brows pursed showing she didn't understand. "You lost me, Eddie. My life with you was full and content."

"But childless." Eddie sighed. "We may've been a great couple together, enjoyed the same things and were the best of friends, in bed and out. But we weren't the right combination to make kids and I knew you wanted them."

Lynn tried to lower her gaze but he didn't let her. His ice-cold touch to her chin made her lift her face to look upon him again. "I knew, Lynn. I always knew."

"It wasn't important." Lynn hurriedly replied. "We had each other."

"That was fine for then, but this is now," Eddie informed her gently before shooting a glance toward the heavens as if someone above had spoken to him. "I gotta make this quick. Seems you made a friend with a ghost named Jasper." She nodded and Eddie continued. "He told me you've been wanting to speak with me. "

"Eddie, I love you," she sputtered. "I miss you so much. There are so many questions that I can't think straight and sort them out to ask."

"You don't have to ask," he said. "I'm safe and happy. I want you to be happy, too. My years with you were the most precious of my life. Our time together was perfect. I've watched over you in your time of need and never left your side when you were down."

"I know," she whispered. "I felt your presence. Why couldn't I see you or speak to you until now?"

"Because you sought me out of desperation," Eddie explained. "When you seek something too hard, your vision becomes dark and cloudy, obscuring the very thing you wish to find. I was there. I've always been there. It took time for you to relax and reach out to me out of love and not the fear of being alone."

Lynn digested his words. He was right. She'd wanted to find him so desperately she'd overlooked the signs he was with her all along. In her heart, she'd known he comforted her when she was down, but her despair and loneliness blocked him from her eyesight. "I've been a fool."

"No, not a fool," Eddie said. "Just scared of being alone. You don't have to be alone any longer. I want you to believe our love of the supernatural helped prepare you for your future."

"My future?"

"Yes," Eddie continued with a nod toward the bed. "Your future if you choose to accept it lays waiting in the other room."

Lynn's heart skipped a beat. "You mean with Padon?"

He nodded as he asked, "Do you love him?"

She thought for a moment. This was something she suspected but hadn't been ready to accept. It seemed to have happened so fast.

"Love knows no boundaries or time constraints," Eddie proclaimed and it astounded her he knew her thoughts just like Jasper had. It had to be a ghost thing.

Taking a leap into the unknown, Lynn admitted, "Yes. I love him."

Eddie kissed her cheek and she shivered from head to toe. "I know you do. Now go in there and make love to him while the sun is rising."

In a flash of light and bright colorful stars, he was gone. Lynn wiped a tear from her eye as she whispered, "I will always love you, Eddie."

"And I you," returned to her on a whisper from the heavens. "Your heart is ready to love again. So go, ride that sexy spontaneity wave into the future. Make me proud."

With the next change of color in the sky, Lynn's laughter at Eddie's spontaneity reference died and she froze as something else he said blazed bright inside her brain. What did he mean by make love to Padon while the sun rose? Then it hit her. Akira's strange words from earlier in the evening replayed in her head.

May thy morning bring ye love for it be love which enlightens thy heart.

Fin's words wafted through her head as well. *Let the heart guide you and your spirit shall be free.*

Bits and pieces from conversations throughout the night scrolled behind her eyes like a stock exchange ticker tape. OhMyGod! They'd been giving them the answer to the curse in roundabout ways, but neither of them had been smart enough to decipher their cryptic messages.

Until now. Thinking back, she felt like such a fool. The answer had been in her heart all along and she'd been too blinded by her desire to locate Eddie to see it. She raised her eyes heavenward and issued a prayer she knew he'd hear.

"Thank you, Eddie."

Lynn ran, dropping the towel in her wake and dove onto the bed. Padon's eyes sprang open as she kissed him. With both hands, she grabbed him, even semi-soft he felt wonderful in her hand. He responded instantly, getting harder with each stroke. Oh Lordy, she loved this man and the way he reacted to her touch.

Padon broke from their kiss and captured her hands. It didn't stop her. Using his grip on her wrists as leverage, she straddled his hips and seated herself on his newly sprung erection. He let go of her hands and followed her pace.

"My wee one, ye have a strong appetite," he practically growled as he met her pump for pump.

In a panic to beat the clock and the sun, she rode him faster and faster, until she almost couldn't breathe and her insides gushed her orgasm. Lynn gasped, "Padon, I love you."

His hands circled her waist and rolled them so he hovered over her with his shaft buried to the hilt. "And I love ye, my wee one. Ye hath been my salvation during my hours o' cursed daylight. A vision o' ye lingers in my head and ye live within my heart to keep me sane when I cannot move to touch ye until nightfall."

She was his salvation. He thought of her while lying cursed within the stone. Lynn kissed him with every ounce of the love she felt in her heart. Padon hugged her tight and devoured her mouth as he glided slowly in and out of her. The tension built in her core and readied her for another round of lovemaking Padon style.

He nibbled her lips, her chin then attacked her nipples, licking and sucking from one to another as if not wanting to cherish one more than the other. He paid them equal affection. Lynn wiggled beneath him. The intensity of his touches made her skin tingle sending tiny pulses of need deep within her.

When Padon increased their pace, Lynn matched it. Lifting off the mattress, grinding into him, taking him as deep as she could possibly take him. She gripped his shaft with her inner muscles stroking him with each pass in and out. He groaned and she knew they both were so close to coming, again. Over and over, faster and faster until sweat beaded off them. Their bodies glistened in the sunlight. Lynn's eyes widened as their orgasms hit taking them both over the edge.

She screamed in ecstasy and joy. Tears flowed freely as she showered his face with kisses. "Padon." She kissed him. "Padon."

She kissed him again and again too happy to speak.

Padon's chest hurt. A pain like no other gripped his heart and squeezed as if a fist held tight trying to explode it. He couldn't take a full breath. Streaks of white-hot spears shot through every inch of him to the point he thought he'd shatter. Stars shot behind his eyes. He was changing, turning to stone while connected with Lynn. He'd crush her. Worse. Would she turn to stone with him if they continued to touch? He knew he had to move quickly. There was no way he'd allow her to suffer the curse with him.

He caught her face in his hands and brushed a hasty kiss to her lips as he quickly rolled off her, placing a decent gap between them. "Lynn, my wee one, I love ye. But—"

Whatever he was going to say was lost as his expression switched to sheer surprise and wonder. He shoved from the bed to stand in the morning sun streaming through the open balcony door. Holding his hands in front of him, he stared at them as if they weren't real. He spun around to face her.

"How?" His brows bunched with his utterly confused question.

Lynn laughed as she sprang from the bed and took his hands in hers. She led him out on the balcony and into the full sunlight. Reaching up, she cupped his cheek.

"Love set you free."

He caught her wrist and kissed her palm, tugging her into a hearty hug. He gathered her in his arms and spun around in the sunshine. Holding her close, Padon kissed her nose, smiling down at her.

"Aye, my wee one. Love hath set me free and ye are my salvation and the keeper o' my heart."

Lynn grinned and waggled her eyebrows at him. "Ever made love on the balcony?"

"Not 'til now."

* * * * *

A flash of light appeared in Gavin and Ericka's bedchamber. Gavin sat upright as did Ericka. She snuggled close to Gavin. Her eyes wide and the sound of her voice was filled with hope. "Good news?"

"Well?" Gavin questioned.

Akira grinned. "Seems there be another *brathair* free."

The end… Until the next brother is found☺

ABOUT THE AUTHOR

Tara Nina creates in a variety of ranges from steamy hot to simmering sweet, which includes paranormals, contemporaries, suspense and sci-fi. She's a Southerner living in the northern wilds of New Jersey complete with grown children, two dogs, six turtles and a mountain man for a husband.

She loves to hear from readers so feel free to contact her via email tara@taranina.com

Please don't get discouraged if it takes a little while before she responds. Unfortunately, she hasn't hit the lottery yet and has to work to battle the bills of home ownership. Being a full-time writer is on her bucket list and one day, she hopes to achieve that goal.

Join her Clan MacKinnon Fan Club/Newsletter for updates on what's new and exciting in her world. http://taranina.com/join-the-clan/

Check out her website http://taranina.com

She is also available on the following media outlets:

Facebook: https://www.facebook.com/TaraNinaAuthor

Twitter: https://twitter.com/taranina

Pinterest: https://www.pinterest.com/taranina/

Instagram: https://www.instagram.com/taranina1

<u>Books by Tara Nina</u>

Cursed MacKinnon's series:
Curse of the Gargoyle (book 1)
Eyes of Stone (book 2)
Cursed Laird (book 3)
Haunted Laird (book 4)

All I Want for Christmas is a Marine

Mountain Men: Brothers Dupree ~ Trilogy

Mindwarp

Playing Cowboy

Candygram

Excerpt
Candygram
Tara Nina

The telescope nearly toppled over in his excitement. Jonah Cambridge readjusted his eye on the scope as he watched the spectacular view in the sky. His hunch was right. He knew what he saw wasn't a typical light show of stars and such. One of those bright spots separated from the main group and spiraled to the ground. Aliens used the meteor shower as a cover for landing on Earth.

He watched its spectacular descent and noted its angulations and trajectory. Using the settings on his high-powered scope, he estimated its distance and guesstimated its rate of speed, then calculated the approximate coordinates of its possible landing site. Once he had the information needed, he scooted his rocking chair away from the telescope. He rocked while he made his calculations. His hand shook as he deduced the radius of the area to be searched. Excitement flowed. If he was right, the landing site was somewhere within town limits.

"Aliens, aliens have landed," he muttered as he plotted the information in the logbook he kept on alien spacecraft he'd seen in the last few years.

"They've landed again, have they? Where at this time, Grandpa?"

Jonah didn't look up from his notations. "I know what I saw. Something came to Earth during that meteor shower and I'm going to prove it."

He stood, closed his logbook and tucked it under his arm. Grabbing his cane, he toddled around his grandson, crossed the wide porch and ambled into the old country-style house through the screen door. The aliens weren't going to out-smart him this time. No, they weren't. He had a fix on them and this time he was going to catch one of those outer space creatures.

"Just remember," Everett stated calmly not wanting to rile his Grandpa. "You are not to be within three hundred feet of the Lane farm. They didn't take kindly to you traipsing through their chicken coup and disturbing their laying hens."

Grandpa turned towards Everett. His cheeks reddened as he shook his cane in the air. The shadowy green eyes that once were bright and matched Everett's seemed to darken with anger. His wildly unkempt, gray hair framed his weathered face, adding a demented flair to his appearance. "I know one of those eggs was really a spaceship. I tell you. Damn alien lovers!"

Everett grinned into his cup before he took a sip, while watching the frail gentleman disappear into the kitchen. This alien obsession was going to be the death of Grandpa. Every star that twinkled funny as far as Grandpa was concerned was an alien spacecraft hovering overhead, spying on Earth.

He shook his head. The former doctor was now simply an old man with a crazy mentality and too much time on his hands. But Everett loved him anyway.

Gotta find Grandpa a different hobby.

Everett turned, walked to the steps, and took a seat on the third one from the top. Staring at the clear night sky, he understood his Grandpa's obsession with the stars, but not his alien theories. He leaned back on his elbows, rested on the edge of the porch, while holding his cup in one hand. Nothing was more relaxing than sitting here, stargazing. Thanks to Grandpa, he'd been doing it since he was old enough to walk. The two of them would sit for hours, peeking through a telescope and discussing the constellations.

But somehow, their hobby corroded grandpa's brain. Everett took another sip. *Aliens did this. Aliens did that.* Grandpa's words whispered through his ears. It was sad to see such a wonderful man slip into this confused state of mind. And it had only gotten worse after Grandma died two years ago.

Everett smiled. Now Lucy Cambridge was a woman who could straighten up Jonah and keep him in line. She had for fifty-three years, before she passed away. He stared into his cup before taking the last swallow. Unfortunately, she wasn't around and the task of keeping tabs on Grandpa had fallen to Everett. Taking over his Grandpa's practice as Port Clef's only doctor gave him a great excuse to move back home and leave the big city behind.

Starting over.

That's exactly what he needed. A slower pace, friendly people and the hometown he missed were the answer to what ailed him. Everett relaxed at the thought. He had a great deal of respect for the doctors and the practice he left behind in New York City. But it never filled that one little void he felt resided inside him for small town life. The women he met there had no desire to leave the hot mess of tall buildings, traffic congestion and wall-to-wall people.

But he did.

He loved this old house with its wraparound porch, its view of the ocean and the crazy old man that came with it. The fact it was located a few miles west of town near the point made it conveniently located to the clinic. Everett stretched his legs and resituated on the steps. He breathed his fill of the salt-water smell lingering on the breeze.

This was home.

www.ingramcontent.com/pod-product-compliance
Lightning Source LLC
Chambersburg PA
CBHW021135110726
47900CB00002B/367

* 9 7 8 1 7 3 4 2 0 5 7 7 0 *